Voyageur

Dan Bomkamp

Lovstad Publishing
Poynette, Wisconsin
Lovstadpublishing@live.com

ISBN: 0692491015
ISBN-13: 978-0692491010
Previous ISBN: 0-9749058-3-6

Printed in the United States of America

Cover: design by Lovstad Publishing; photo by Dan Bomkamp.
Thanks to Tony Chitwood, Jackson Young, and Brandon Harris
for portraying the characters Ladd, Willie, and Tone.

For Mom.

ACKNOWLEDGMENTS

There are many people I wish to thank for their help in writing this book.

One is Meg Galloway of the Wisconsin DNR. She did an outstanding job researching information on the Wisconsin River dams as they were in 1914.

The staff at the Spring Green, Wisconsin Public Library was very helpful in researching the historic events portrayed in this book.

Webster's Dictionary defines an editor as "one who alters matter for publication to make it more suitable." I wish to thank my Editor and friend Joel Lovstad for his work on *Voyageur*. He not only made it more suitable for publication, he transformed my somewhat plebeian and clumsy prose into a work that makes me look like a much better writer than I am.

And I want to thank the late Ladd Rut, an "old timer" who was a wonderful storyteller. He was a hunter, trapper, fisherman and outdoorsman his whole life, and he spent countless hours on the Wisconsin River and its sloughs. I enjoyed many hours listening to his enthralling stories of the old days. His tales gave me the original idea for this book. I hope my telling of this story will entertain my readers as Ladd entertained me.

Voyageur

Prolog

June 1673

Seven men sweated profusely as they neared the end of their portage on the banks of the small stream. Strong, tough men accustomed to hard work, they were brave enough to set out into unexplored country. They were *The Voyageurs*. Their leader: a Jesuit Priest, Father Jacques Marquette; second in command was Pierre Joliet, a French mapmaker. The local Indians had told them of this river, and that it flowed to the west where it met a larger river. This excited the explorers. They were looking for a passage to the Pacific Ocean, and this just might be the route they were searching for.

The journey along the eastern shoreline of Lake Michigan had taken nearly two weeks. They had stayed close to the shore to avoid the swells and waves of the huge lake, and when they rounded the peninsula that would one day be called Door County, they paddled along its western shore into Green Bay. After several days of exploration and some days to rest, they had started up the Fox River, and now they were about to set out on their greatest quest—to find the passage to the Pacific Ocean.

They loaded their gear into the canoes and began a journey that would take them over 450 miles down the *Mescousing*, the name the Indians had given to this small river. As the river flowed southwestward, it ran through steep banks and sheer cliffs and the current was fast and the water deep. When they had traveled for many days, the river widened and became shallow, dotted with sandbars and islands.

Along the way they saw marvelous things. Wildlife abounded; deer and bison roamed in great herds; ducks, geese and many other birds inhabited the trees and marshes. The land was a vast expanse of hills, plains and forests—a wonderful place with much fertile soil and many friendly people.

After weeks of travel they entered the Mississippi near the place where a trading post called *Prairie du Chien* would one day be established. Traveling down the Mississippi for many more miles, they finally accepted the fact that this was not the way to the Pacific.

Though they didn't find the passage to the Pacific Ocean, they were the first to explore the Wisconsin River. Father Marquette and Pierre Joliet had no idea that their journey would put their names into the history books as *The Voyageurs*—the discoverers of the Wisconsin River—*"the Stream of a Thousand Isles."*

Voyageur

Voyageur

DAN BOMKAMP

Chapter 1

Spring 1913

My given name is Galahad. My mother, Ellen, is an English and Literature teacher at our local high school. During the latter days of her pregnancy, she read a book about Camelot, King Arthur and the Knights of the Round Table. These gallant characters and the romantic stories of heroism and bravery and the illicit love affair between Queen Gwinevere and the handsome Lancelot enthralled her. Galahad, who was the son of Lancelot, must have struck her fancy because good old Mom stuck me with the name, Galahad Arthur Larson. Shortly after my birth, my father convinced her that Galahad was a little flowery for a small town boy and talked her into a little shorter nickname for me. Consequently I grew up to be called Ladd Larson.

Mom read the Classics to me from the time I was old enough to remember. Books like *Moby Dick, A Tale of Two Cities,* and *David Copperfield,* were standard reading at our house. Every night at bedtime she read to me – the stories of the days of old. It is no wonder that as I got old enough to read on my own, I spent much of my free time reliving the adventures of these classic story heroes.

My dad, Eric, is a carpenter and cabinetmaker. He has a workshop behind our house, and even though we live in a small town, he has enough work to keep him busy all year long, and he has built many of the fine homes in our town. When the weather is cold he works in his shop crafting kitchen cabinets, doors and furniture for houses that he will build during the warmer months.

Our next-door neighbors, the Trinchi's, are our best friends.

Their son Marcus Antonius, or Tone as we call him, (pronounced Tony) and I are only just a bit over one day apart in age – I was born just a few minutes before midnight and Tone was born just a few minutes after midnight one day later. Our mothers were pregnant together, almost managed to deliver their babies on the same day and essentially Tone and I grew up like brothers. I slept in Tone's crib and he in mine when one of our mothers was baby sitting while the other ran errands or worked. As a baby I spent my days at Tone's house while my mom was at school. He spent his evenings at my house while his mother, Angela, ran the kitchen and was the head cook in the Smalley House hotel. So Tone and I have spent most of our lives together. We took our first steps together, learned our first words, started school together and have always been best of friends. We often know what each other is thinking and act on things without even talking – something like the bond between twins.

Tone's dad, Robert, is a mason and carpenter and works with my dad on the new houses, and does repair work on existing homes. Robert is a very good designer, too, and draws the plans for many of the jobs that he and Dad work on together. Our mothers are best friends, and our fathers are best friends, so it's no surprise that Tone and I are best friends, too.

We have celebrated our birthdays together ever since our first one. But instead of celebrating my birthday and then celebrating Tone's birthday two days later, we celebrate on the day between. For me it's a day late and for Tone it's a day early, but instead of two little parties, our families get together and we have one big bash. Tone and I have just finished our 10th grade school year, and if everything goes as planned this summer, we will be spending the next summer living on an island in the river. It will be our last year before we finish school and get jobs, and probably our last summer together, so we want to make some money during this school vacation to finance a real adventure next year.

Our plan is to build a cabin on an island in the river and to spend the summer there, fishing and living off the land. We've both been saving our money from working at odd jobs for the past three summers, and we've studied hard in school and have gotten good grades, so our parents have tentatively agreed to our plan. We brought up the idea a couple of years ago and have kept working them toward approval. So far we have "probably" as an answer, so that's good enough for us. This summer we have to gather up all the materials for our cabin and make enough money to buy the stuff we need for the exploit and then we'll be ready for our last great adventure together.

Chapter 2

After fifteen years together, Tone and I are still like brothers. We played together as toddlers, started school together, moved up through the grades and now we are nearly finished with high school. We've spent more time together than most real brothers. We learned how to talk, write, swim, fish, and in the past few years we've learned a little about girls. Everyone thinks of us as LaddandTone – not like two people, but more like one. Wherever one of us is, the other is. But as similar as we are in everything, there is no problem knowing who is who.

Tone's family is second generation Italian. His grandparents on his dad's side emigrated here over thirty years ago from a small town called Rieti, near Rome. His mom's parents arrived in the area a few years later and both families farmed a short distance from town. His dad and mom were childhood sweethearts, married and moved to town right next door to my parents.

Tone certainly has his family's features: dark complexion and black wavy hair. But instead of brown eyes like most Italians, he has the deepest blue eyes that I've ever seen. His mom says that somewhere in their ancestry there must be a Norwegian Viking who passed on the genes for blue eyes. Over the generations, there has been the occasional blue-eyed family member, and

Tone just happens to be one of them. The girls just go batty over his long, black curls, his long, dark eyelashes, and that dazzling wide smile.

The story of my Norwegian parents and ancestors is pretty much the same. My grandparents on both sides of the family are farmers in the area, too, and when my dad was in school, he found that he was really talented in the building trade, and he thought that life as a carpenter would be better than struggling on a farm. When he married mom, she made it clear that she would be a teacher and that they would need to live in town, so they moved into our house just a few weeks before Tone's family moved into the house next door.

My inherited Scandinavian features are quite opposite from Tone's. But other than my light brown hair that isn't as wavy, and my Scandinavian blue eyes, and the fact that I'm just an inch or so taller, we're like twins. We're almost exactly the same size, and we even wear the same size shoe. We trade clothes often, and our moms have just about given up trying to figure out which clothes belong where.

We began talking about spending a summer on the river when Mom brought a book home to me and I was reading aloud to Tone about the travels of the Voyageurs – Father Marquette and Pierre Joliet. We usually took turns reading these adventure stories and we've read many books together. It was exciting to imagine the journey of those first explorers of these lands. There were no roads, no houses, and no other people except the Indians. We marveled at the bravery of those first ventures into a completely unknown territory.

Tone and I talked many hours about what it would be like to travel just as the explorers did and live off the land. Soon the idea of spending a summer on the river took root. The more we talked about it the more excited we became, and we began making plans. We needed to gather up enough lumber to build a small cabin; we would need to buy or build a boat so we could get up and down the river. And of course, we would need groceries, so we formulated a plan that involved catching fish and bringing them to town to barter for supplies from Mr. Marcus, the local general store owner.

Our idea got a big boost when my dad asked us if we wanted to help him tear down an old summer kitchen on a lot where he would build a new house.

"What are you going to do with the old lumber?" I asked Dad.

"I suppose most of it'll be just junk, so we'll burn it," he said.

Tone and I exchanged glances. We both beamed with the same idea. "If we tear it down, can we have the lumber?"

"What for?" Dad asked.

We told him that instead of just wrecking the summer kitchen, we'd take it apart carefully so we could re-use a lot of the lumber for our cabin on the river. We even thought we would use the roofing if we could save it.

"So you're sure your mothers are going along with this summer on the island?"

"They said it was alright. I'd think that it's still okay," I said.

"I'll talk to your moms just to make sure before you go through all the trouble, and then finding out that they've changed their minds," Dad said.

We could hardly contain ourselves for the next few days. Finally, four days later Mom said, "So, if I let you build this cabin and spend the summer on the river, you'll be careful?"

"Of course, Mom. You know us. We're always careful."

"I guess you two have good heads on your shoulders. You've never gotten into trouble... yet." She gave me a long look. "Okay, I guess it's alright with me."

I jumped up joyously and gave Mom a big hug. "Thanks, Mom," I blurted, and without further discussion I ran out the door, heading across the yard for Tone's house. I could hardly wait to announce the good news. I knocked once like I always did, opened the door and ran smack into Tone who was on his way out. I could see the excitement in his eyes.

"My mom said yes!" Tone blurted before I could say a word.

"Mine too!" I answered.

We grabbed each other and began dancing around the kitchen.

"Hey, hey, you two! Don't knock down my house," Tone's mom scolded, but laughing at us, too.

"Sorry, Mom."

"Yeah, sorry," I said. We bolted for the door and ran to my dad's shop.

Dad was grinning as we came flying through the door. "I see you've talked to your moms."

"Thanks a million, Dad," I said.

"Yeah, thanks! Boy oh boy, thanks," Tone added.

"So what's the decision on the summer kitchen?" Dad asked.

"We'll tear it down, and if it's okay we'll save as much of the lumber as we can for the cabin."

"Okay. I'll pay you a dollar each and you can have the lumber," Dad said, and then he added a bonus to the deal. "Oh, and by the way, there's a cook stove in the summer kitchen. You can have that, too, if you can find a way to get it to the island."

"We'll find a way, Dad."

Chapter 3

D ad took Tone and me to the lot where the summer kitchen stood and showed us around. The main house had burned down the previous winter and the owners wanted Dad to replace it with a larger house. There wasn't enough space on the lot for the summer kitchen, so it had to go.

Summer kitchens had always been a common sight at most homes in our town. For those who could afford them and had sufficient room on their lot, the summer kitchen provided a place outside the main house to cook meals and can garden vegetables during the warm months, keeping all that heat out of the house. But the summer kitchens were losing their popularity, as most new houses were built with better kitchens right in the main structure. The summer kitchen was becoming a thing of the past.

"The corrugated roof tin is good on this one," Dad said, "and if you're careful, I think you can save it and most of the lumber. How big is this cabin you're planning?"

"Not nearly this big," I said. "We're planning on just a place to eat and sleep and to get in out of the rain. We're thinking maybe about ten feet square."

"Well, then. There's plenty of material here. If there's some lumber left that you don't need, I can always find a use for it."

We went back home and loaded some tools onto the small wagon and hitched up Carl, one of our horses, and then Tone and I returned to begin dismantling the building. We started with the roof tin. Removing it was a pretty simple job that just took a little patience. We had a lot of nails to pull and had to be careful not to tear any large holes in the material. In a short while, we had all the tin stacked up and ready to haul away.

Then the roof boards came off and the rafters came down, and in about three weeks time, there was nothing left but the floor and foundation. We had several stacks of lumber – a pile of two by fours and another pile of two by sixes. There were planks for wall sheathing and beams for the roof. As we dismantled the building we pulled all of the nails from the wood so it was ready to use again. We saved the door and a window and a couple of cabinets. Working around the stove, we left it standing on the floor, and that was all that was left of the summer kitchen.

There was no way the two of us could lift the stove onto the wagon. While it wasn't one of the biggest stoves, it weighed a lot more than we could lift. We thought we could slide the stove up on a couple of planks, but it didn't take long to find out that it was still more than we could handle alone, so we recruited a few of our friends. We needed two more strong guys to help push the stove and one to keep Carl from moving. One of our neighbor boys, Willie, was about twelve. He was kind of skinny and wouldn't be of much help pushing, but he could hold Carl steady. We talked two of our friends from school into helping us push. Willie held Carl's harness and talked to him to keep him from getting nervous, while the other two guys and Tone and I drug the stove over behind the wagon and started sliding it up the planks. The planks sagged and made cracking sounds under the weight of the stove, but we managed to slide it up and finally got it into the wagon. The rest of us climbed up in the wagon while Tone climbed up on the seat, took the reins and drove back to our house. We backed the wagon up to the barn, slid the stove down the planks, manhandled it into a corner and covered it with an old canvas for winter storage.

We went back to where the summer kitchen had been and Tone and I began loading up the saved lumber and hauled that back to the barn, too. Little Willie helped us load and haul the lumber home, and he was quite excited when we told him about our island plans for the following summer. The next day we went back and cleaned up the mess and put all the nails and screws that we had pulled from the lumber into cans. Tone and I spent many hours that winter sorting and straightening nails, hammering them on an old piece of railroad iron, so we could use them for building our cabin.

Dad came to the building site with us the next day. We

poured kerosene on the floor and burned it up. When the fire was out and things had cooled down the next day, Tone and I beat the foundation to pieces with mauls and threw all of the stones and cement down into a root cellar that had been under the old summer kitchen. We shoveled all the ashes in, and then finished filling the hole with dirt and smoothed it over. The summer kitchen was no more. In a few weeks, you would have to look hard to tell where it had been.

That job took most of our summer, but we had all the lumber we needed for our cabin, plus a window, a door and a stove. We had our roofing material and all the nails we would need, plus there were two dollars more in our cabin fund. Our dream was beginning to take shape.

Chapter 4

Tone and I are gravediggers. It's not a job that we expected to have, or one that we went looking for – the job sort of found us. We've had the job for the past two years, ever since the former gravedigger, Harlan Pratt, was found lying dead in a nearly finished grave. Harlan was an old guy who dug the graves, unloaded shipments of caskets, and helped Mr. DeSilva, the undertaker, to place the deceased into their casket when the embalming was finished.

Harlan had a great love for rye whiskey with a beer chaser. He had an overly healthy appetite for big steaks and lots of gravy, too. And then there were the big, smelly cigars that he puffed on from the time he woke up each morning until he went to bed at night. All those things were hard on his heart. Add a hot, humid spring morning to his heart problems and Harlan's vices finally got the best of him. Mr. DeSilva became concerned one day when Harlan didn't come back to the funeral home when he should have, so he drove his buggy down to the cemetery. There he found poor Harlan lying dead as a doornail in the bottom of the grave he had just dug – the stub of his unlit cigar still clenched tightly between his teeth.

There was a funeral the next day, so Mr. DeSilva stopped by our house and asked my dad if he thought Tone and I would be interested in helping him out. He needed someone to fill in the grave that Harlan had dug, once its occupant had taken residency. He also needed someone to dig all the graves from then on, beginning with one for Harlan. The job paid a dollar per grave, and he even offered to give us the dollar that Harlan would have been paid had he lived to finish the job. Of course, Tone and I jumped at the idea. Two dollars was a fortune to us.

First we had to go with Mr. DeSilva to the cemetery to get Harlan out of the hole he was occupying. Both Tone and I had to jump down into the hole with Harlan, and after much grunting and groaning, we managed to get him up to where Mr. DeSilva could grab his arms. It was like pushing a rope uphill. Tone climbed out of the hole while I held onto Harlan so he wouldn't slide back to the bottom again, and then by me pushing and Tone and Mr. DeSilva pulling, we got Harlan out and loaded him up on the wagon.

From then on, Tone and I were the official gravediggers. We dug graves for several of the small country churches, too, that had their own cemeteries. For graves in town, we earned a dollar. Our town being in the river valley, the ground is mostly sand and it's real easy digging. Tone and I could usually dig a grave in two or three hours, and to fill it back in took less than an hour, so we were making a great hourly wage.

The cemeteries in the country were a little different. The ground was heavy – usually clay and rock. They didn't want to make a cemetery right in the middle of good, flat farmland, so they usually ended up somewhere on the side of a hill where nothing would grow anyway. After we spent nearly ten hours on the first of these country church graves, digging out boulders, we told Mr. DeSilva that we wanted more money for the out-of-town graves. He agreed to $1.25.

The day after we dug Harlan's grave, Mr. DeSilva needed help to move his body. He came to my house and asked if we could give him a hand. We didn't think much about it and both rode over to the funeral home with him in his buggy.

When we walked into the embalming room, we both stopped short. There lying on the big metal table was the mortal remains of poor Harlan. Now, we had seen Harlan dead, but now he was naked as the day he was born, and there were incisions where Mr. DeSilva had sucked out his blood and replaced it with embalming fluid. Harlan's skin was really white and pasty looking, and the smell of the embalming fluid nearly made us lose our breakfast.

A casket on a little metal cart with wheels was parked right next to the table.

"One of you take his feet and the other take his shoulders. Lift him carefully into the casket," Mr. DeSilva said. "You must be careful to keep him level, and for God's sake, don't drop him."

I looked at Tone. His usually dark, handsome face was stark white as he stared at poor old Harlan.

"Which end do you want, Tone?" I asked.

Tone swallowed. "I'll... I'll take his feet... I guess."

I moved to the head end of the table and Tone went to the foot end, and we both stood there gawking at Harlan as if we were expecting him to move over to the casket on his own.

"You've got to pick him up, boys. He's not going to bite you. He's quite dead."

"So, we just kind of slide him off the table and into the casket?" I asked.

"Yup. He's stiff as a board so he won't bend, but you must keep him level. We don't want the embalming fluid to run out. That's why I need helpers. I can't keep him level by myself."

We got into position. "Are you ready?" I asked Tone. He nodded.

I took hold of Harlan's shoulders and Tone took hold of his ankles. His skin felt like cold bread dough. We both lifted and slid Harlan off the table and laid him in the casket. Then Mr. DeSilva raised the casket up higher so he could dress Harlan and finish getting him ready for the funeral.

"Now, we wouldn't want to send Harlan to the Pearly Gates naked. I'll put some clothes on him now." We noticed that Harlan's clothes were all slit up the back. He laid some underwear on Harlan and tucked them under on the sides, and then he began putting on the shirt and pants in the same way.

"I wondered how you were going to do that," Tone said.

"Nothing to it," Mr. DeSilva said. "Thanks for the help." He tossed each of us a quarter.

"Thank you, sir," we said, and out the door we went. When we got outside Tone headed for a shade tree and sat down. "Wow, that was something, wasn't it?"

"Yeah, it didn't seem so bad when he was in the hole and had clothes on, but to see him all naked and white looking – that was pretty nasty," I said.

"Well, I guess Mr. DeSilva was right. He didn't bite us, so what the heck?"

Tone tossed his quarter in the air and caught it. "Easiest two bits I've ever made, though," he said.

After that, we were Mr. DeSilva's regular helpers. We carried bodies from the hearse to the embalming room, helped move them from the slab to the casket, and in time, the dead bodies didn't bother us so much. The money was good, and every dead body made our financial situation just a little better.

Chapter 5

Tone and I were lounging in his room, talking about our cabin and trying to figure out how we were going to get the stove and lumber to the island. Of course, we wouldn't be moving to the island until next year after we had finished eleventh grade. But we liked to talk about it and make plans.

There came a knock at the front door. Tone ran downstairs to answer it. "Hey Ladd! Come down here," he yelled up the stairs to me.

I went down to see Willie standing at the door. Tone said, "Willie says that Mr. DeSilva sent him over to get us. He has some work for us to do."

Willie nodded, and then he added, "He's got a big wagonload of caskets from some place up north, and the guy driving the wagon needs help to unload them. He said to get over there pronto!"

We hurried down the street to the Funeral Home. A huge wagon hitched to a team of six horses waited at the rear of the building. Mr. DeSilva was talking to the teamster as we walked up.

"Here they are," he said, as we came near. "I told you they'd be here as soon as Willie found them." He tossed a nickel in the air. Willie grabbed it and stuck it in his pocket.

"Boys, this fella is delivering my load of caskets. He and I are getting a little long in the tooth to be hauling all of these heavy things into the Funeral Home, so I was hoping you two would unload them for us."

"We'll be glad to, Mr. DeSilva," I said.

"Be real careful with the ones in the packing crates. They're fancy... and expensive," Mr. DeSilva explained. "They're packed in straw to keep them from getting scratched. When you get them out of the crates, wipe them clean and take them into the casket room."

The casket room was Mr. DeSilva's showroom that displayed all the different kinds of caskets where the relatives of the deceased could select the one they wanted. There were really fancy ones covered with copper and tin and brass that had been hammered into pretty designs and then polished to a shiny finish. Some were just wood for those who couldn't afford such luxury for their final rest.

Mr. DeSilva continued his instructions: "There are two or three of some, so put one in the casket room and the rest in the garage. Mr. Honer and I are going up to the hotel in the meantime and have a cold Sarsaparilla." He winked at us, and we knew his Sarsaparilla was probably going to be a shot of rye whiskey and a beer to chase it down.

Mr. Honer was a big man with huge muscular arms and strong hands. A merry twinkle flashed in his eye and he laughed when Mr. DeSilva said they were going for Sarsaparilla. "Thanks for the help, boys, and thank you young Willie for fetching them for us." He tousled Willie's mop of blonde hair.

"You're welcome, sir."

Mr. Honer and Mr. DeSilva ambled off down the street. We removed the tarp covering the cargo and then began unloading the wagon. In an hour or so we were finished. Willie helped us; when we uncrated the fancy caskets, he removed all the straw and wiped off the dust. All the while we worked he chattered about his sisters and how they tormented him, and that he was going to run away and join the circus as soon as he had some money saved up. He was a cute kid and we enjoyed his entertaining conversation.

We had six empty wooden crates stacked up in the yard and we didn't know for sure what to do with them. Just then Mr. DeSilva and Mr. Honer came walking down the street, laughing and acting as if they had had more than one Sarsaparilla.

"Mr. DeSilva, what should we do with these crates?" I asked.

"Take them out back and bust them up. Put them in a pile and burn them," he said.

Tone and I began carrying the crates around to the back of the garage and I picked up a crowbar. Just as I was about to start smashing the crates, I had an idea. "Hey Tone! What do you think of building a boat with some of this lumber? We need a way to get out to our island, and if we had a boat we could row up and down the river and do all kinds of stuff. I'll bet we could row back to town a lot faster than we could walk, too. The planks in these boxes could make a boat, and they're free."

"Yeah, that's a great idea. And if we have a boat we can put out set lines for fishing and do a lot more exploring."

We told Mr. DeSilva that we'd like to take the crates home to use them for a project that we were working on.

"You're welcome to them, and thanks for getting right over here and unloading that wagon," he said. He handed us each two quarters.

"I'm about ready to leave, boys," Mr. Honer said. "Throw those crates back up on the wagon and I'll haul them over to your house for you."

We loaded up the crates and thanked Mr. DeSilva. Mr. Honer drove over to our house and stopped by the barn. On the way, Willie sat up on the seat with Mr. Honer and told him a bunch of tall tales. You could tell that Mr. Honer was enjoying himself as he burst out laughing many times as we rolled down the street. Tone and I unloaded the crates and thanked Mr. Honer for the lift.

"You're more than welcome, boys. It was a pleasure meeting

you," he said. "Well, young Willie, I'll drop you off at your house if you'd like. I'm going right past it."

"Thanks, Mr. Honer," Willie beamed. "See you guys later." He waved and grinned as they drove off.

Tone smiled as he watched Willie go down the street with Mr. Honer. "He's a funny little shit. I like him."

I had to agree with him on that.

We stood there a few moments gazing at our newfound treasure. "Well, the next step is to tear these things apart," I said, "and to figure out how to build a boat." That might take more skill than we had, but we knew some guys who were talented woodworkers, and one of them was good at making scale drawings. Dad and Robert would be our next stop.

Chapter 6

Mom was standing at the sink peeling potatoes when Tone and I walked into the kitchen.

"Hi Mom," I said, and gave her a kiss on the cheek.

"Hi Mom," Tone said and gave her a hug.

Mom turned around and Tone gave her one of his most dazzling smiles and cocked his head off to the side. "Oh, you're my other mom, not my regular mom."

My mom smiled and put her arms around Tone and gave him a hug. "I think you've spent as much of your life here as Laddy has, so I'm happy to be your *other* mom." She reached over and put one arm around me and gave me a kiss on the cheek. "So, what are you two handsome devils up to?"

"What do you mean? Why do you think we're up to something?"

"You guys don't fool me. You want something," she said smiling.

Tone took the paring knife from her hand and began peeling potatoes. "Let me help. By the way – what's for supper?"

She laughed. "Chicken and noodles with mashed potatoes. What kind of vegetable do you guys want?"

"Corn," Tone said.

"Peas," I said.

"Well, then it's corn *and* peas," Mom laughed. "Run down to the cellar and get a jar of each, will you?"

I went to the pantry and opened a trap door to the steep stairs down into the cellar where Mom kept her canned vegetables from the garden. There was a candle in a holder on

23

the wall and a box of matches on the shelf. I lit the candle, illuminating the small, stone walled, sand floored room under the house. There were bins built into one wall that held potatoes, carrots, beets and onions from the garden harvest. On the two side walls there were shelves that held dozens of jars of fruits and vegetables that Mom and Tone's mom had canned. Each fall they canned tomatoes, beans, peas, corn, beets, and made applesauce and tomato juice, and the years when grapes were plentiful, they even made grape juice. There were jars of canned chicken, pork and beef, too. And guarding it all was Tyrone the Toad.

Tyrone had been in the cellar for as long as I could remember. He was the biggest toad I had ever seen, and despite being in the dark basement, he seemed to be thriving. My grandma put him there when I was a little kid, and she said he would eat all the insects that might damage our potatoes and other vegetables. Every few days we put a saucer of water down for him and he seemed as happy as a toad could be.

"Mom, Tyrone needs some water," I yelled up to the kitchen.

"Hand me his saucer and I'll fill it," she replied.

"How's he looking?" Mom asked as she handed the filled saucer back to me.

"He looks fat and happy," I said. I picked up a jar of corn and a jar of peas and said goodbye to Tyrone. I blew out the candle, climbed the stairs, and lowered the trap door. I handed the jars to Mom and said, "Tyrone says hi."

Mom just laughed.

Tone finished peeling the potatoes, and with the pan of peelings, he and I walked back to the barn to give them to the chickens. They went wild for potato peelings.

Both of our families used the barn. We each had a team of horses and rather than build two barns and two corrals, we put the horses in together. There was a small chicken house built onto the south side of the barn and each spring we let a few hens sit on their eggs to hatch about fifty chicks. Then in the fall we had fresh chickens for a while and our moms canned the rest. We always kept enough hens over the winter to keep both families supplied with eggs. Between the chickens and our big gardens, and some ducks, geese, and occasionally a deer, we always had plenty to eat. Quite often, someone who had work for Dad or Robert would barter for a pig or a beef, and then we had fresh meat for a few days. What we didn't eat was canned and added to the rest of the food that we grew. We never had a problem keeping food on the table. Tone and I fished in the river and backwaters a lot in our spare time and so we had fresh fish quite often, too.

While we were standing there throwing peelings to the chickens, Dad and Robert drove up in the wagon.

"Hi, Dad," Tone and I said simultaneously.

"Hi, guys," they said. "What are the crates for?"

"That's something we wanted to talk to you about."

They looked at each other as if they knew we were up to something.

"Oh, it's nothing bad. But maybe it's something that's too difficult for you to do."

"And what might that be?" Dad asked.

"We need someone to help us build a boat. Do you know anyone who knows anything about boats?"

"What kind of boat are you looking for?" Robert asked.

"Whatever kind you think you can design and build." Tone suggested.

"What do you know about building a boat?" I asked my dad.

"A boat? Well, I've never built one," he said, "but I don't think it would be too hard."

"We've been thinking that if we had a boat for next summer, we could use it to haul our lumber and stuff out to the island," Tone added. "And then when we want to fish or come to town, we could just use it to travel up the river instead of walking."

"You're not going to try to haul that stove out in a boat, I hope," Dad said questioningly.

"No, that would take a pretty big boat," I responded. "We

want something that's easy to paddle but will be stable and will go in shallow water. You know how the river can be in the summer."

"I've got an idea for a design," Robert said. "Give me a little time to think about it, and I'll draw something up."

Just then Mom yelled out the back door for us to come to supper. "Robert, you might as well have supper with us, too. Tone is staying, and Angela went to work early. I've got plenty."

My dad slapped Robert on the back and said, "Come on, let's wash up and then after supper we can take a look at that boat idea of yours."

We had a great time during supper talking about Mr. DeSilva and Mr. Honer, and how silly they had acted when they returned from the tavern.

"He sure is a funny guy to have such a somber job," Tone said.

"I suppose that's why he's so jolly," Mom said. "He *has* to be... to keep from getting depressed... with all that death and sorrow around him."

"He's sure been good to us," I said. "We get paid real good and he never yells at us or nothing."

"Get paid *well* and never yells at us or *anything*, honey. Not *nothing*," Mom corrected my poor grammar.

"Ma, jeez! You're not teaching now."

"Mr. DeSilva knows good help when he gets it," Tone's dad said. "And if you guys do a good job, he'll want to keep you."

"Mr. Honer is real nice too," Tone said. "He really took a shine to Willie. Of course, everyone likes Willie."

"He's such a cute little kid," Mom said. "It's so sad that his daddy died and left his mother with all those kids. My goodness – five children and no daddy."

"And poor Willie. The only boy," Dad commented.

Tone and I helped Mom with the dishes. Dad and Robert went to Dad's shop and began working on a plan for our boat. By the time we finished in the kitchen, they had a pretty nice drawing completed and were adding some dimensions to it.

26

"What do you think?" Tone's dad asked.

We looked at the drawing and our eyes just about popped out of our heads. It was a magnificent boat.

"I've never seen such a pretty boat," I said.

"Wow, Dad! That's great! Where did you ever get the idea for such a boat?" Tone asked.

"Remember that picture that Grandma has in her parlor?" Robert quizzed. That's a gondola... in Venice... in Italy. This is just a variation of that."

Indeed, the boat was something that no one in our town had ever seen. Most of the local boats were just rectangular boxes with a couple of seats in them. Some people had canoes, but we didn't want anything so narrow and tippy as a canoe.

Instead of having straight, boxy sides, the sketch of the boat showed sides that curved out in a graceful arc, making the middle about twice as wide as the ends. And, instead of having a bow that narrowed down and a stern that was just square, this boat had what amounted to two bows. Both ends gracefully angled up so that it would slide through the water easily from either end. Two seats, one in each end, were back from the ends far enough so that you could sit facing either direction, and still have legroom to paddle. It looked like a combination of a boat and canoe.

"Dad, it's amazing, but can you build such a boat?" I asked.

"Well, I think with Robert's help we can give it a pretty good try. You guys take those crates apart, pull out all the nails, and then sort the lumber and get it ready for us. Tomorrow evening, when we get back from the building site, we'll see what we can do about making you the best boat on the whole river."

If the boat turned out half as good as it looked on paper, it truly would be a wonderful vessel.

Chapter 7

Tone and I had barely started on the crates the next day when Willie showed up wanting to help. I had never seen Willie's summertime attire vary much from bib overalls cut off to make shorts, shirtless and barefoot. That day was no exception. Just the sight of him – tall, skinny as a rail, a shock of sun-bleached blond hair, sparkling green eyes and smattering of freckles across his nose suggested that he was ready for mischief at a moment's notice.

"Can I help?"

"Sure, Willie. Grab a hammer and you can pull the nails out of the boards as we take the crates apart."

Tone and I began taking the crates apart and Willie seemed quite content with his assigned task. After we had all of the crates dismantled in a couple of hours, we carried the piles of lumber to Dad's cabinet shop. We sorted and stacked them against the back wall, out of the way of Dad's other work.

Robert and Tone came over after supper that evening, and we all went to the shop to start the boat project. Tone and I were anxious to begin the construction, but Robert and Dad were more patient, sorting through the lumber, separating the most perfect boards from the ones with flaws. They'd look down the length of each board and choose the ones with the best grain and look for those that had a little bend in them one way or the other.

I know that Dad and Robert appreciated our attempt to help,

but we were actually more of a hindrance to them. "I don't want to make you guys feel bad, but if you'd get out of the way, we'd make more progress," Dad finally said.

"Sorry, Dad. "We're just kind of anxious for our boat."

"Well, you'd better be patient. This isn't like building some box. It has to float and be water tight, and it'll take at least a month."

A month! We thought we'd have a boat in a couple of days. And what was worse, it was going to be autumn soon and cold weather was coming. How were we going to test the boat before next spring?

"I'll tell you how you guys can help," Dad said. "Take a couple of pails down to the river bottoms tomorrow and look for pine trees that have been blown down or have limbs broken. Chisel off the dried pine pitch where the breaks are. We'll need several pails of pitch to seal the cracks between the boards in the boat."

"We can go right now," I said, excited with the responsibility of an important job.

"No... it'll be dark in an hour," Dad said. "There's no hurry. We won't be sealing it for a quite a while, so just wait till tomorrow."

Dad and Robert could tell that we were disappointed with the length of time required to complete the project.

"You guys are going to have the best boat on the river," Robert said, trying to soothe our anxiety. "So be patient and you'll see... it'll be worth the wait."

"Yeah, I guess you're right," Tone said sorrowfully. It's hard to be patient when you're fifteen years old.

Leaving Dad and Robert to their work, we went to Tone's room and tried to think of some aversion to take our minds off the boat. "Let's make a drawing of our cabin like our dads did with the boat," Tone suggested with a great deal of enthusiasm. "We can decide how to build it and we'll have a plan to go by when we get out there."

We brought out paper, pencils, and a ruler and began

sketching some ideas of the shape and size, and where to put the bed and stove and such. A rough drawing soon took form, and when we were satisfied with the results, we made another drawing to scale. By then it was getting dark and we had to light a lamp to see. I looked at Tone's clock.

"Wow, it's after ten o'clock, I better get home or Mom will skin me."

"See ya in the morning," Tone chuckled.

"Yeah, g'night."

Tone came over in his work clothes first thing the next morning. Before we had finished our breakfast, Willie was at the door. "How's the boat coming?" he asked.

"Have you had breakfast, Willie?" Mom asked. There was a bit of concern in her voice.

"No ma'am," Willie answered with a sheepish smile. "My sisters were all crowded in the kitchen so I just left."

"Well, then. Sit yourself down with the boys and I'll fix you some eggs."

Willie's dazzling smile cheered us all as he slid onto a chair.

"Gonna take at least a month to finish the boat," we told Willie.

"A month! I thought it would be done in a couple of days." He seemed disappointed like we had been.

"Hey Willie, we're going to get some pine pitch for the cracks in the boat. Want to come along and help?"

"Sure, what do I have to do?"

"Just come with us and we'll show you."

I went to the barn and found a bunch of tin buckets and some chisels. We drove Carl along the sand road that runs west from town along the high bank toward the river bottoms until we got into an area that had a lot of pine trees.

At one time water covered our valley from bluff to bluff. But over the centuries, the river got smaller and cut its channel into a narrower area. Now, what once was the riverbank is the high bank that borders the bottoms or sloughs along the river. If you poke around in the sand dunes – some are a half-mile from the river – you will often find clam and snail shells that were left behind when the whole valley was under water. That's always hard to imagine.

The forest along the road was mostly jack pines, white pines, red pines and river birch with a few scrub oaks thrown in here and there. We tied Carl up to a birch tree, walked along the road for a while, and then headed deeper into the woods looking for damaged pine trees.

When a pine tree is struck by lightning, or a limb is broken by the wind, it produces a lot of sticky pitch that covers and seals the injury. As the pitch dries, it turns a yellow color and is as hard as rock candy. And that's what we were searching for.

"Look up there," Tone said pointing to a big white pine. "That whole side is skinned off. There's a ton of pitch on it."

It appeared as though the tree had been struck by lightning; a string of pitch that must have been five feet long clung to a big gouge down one side. "I'll go up and scrape it off," Tone said. He took off his shirt so he wouldn't get pitch all over it. Then he tied one end of a string to the handle of his bucket and the other end to his belt loop. I watched as he climbed the tree, and when he reached the lower end of the tree's injury, he pulled the bucket up and began chipping off the pitch and dropping it into the bucket. "Yuck, it's sticky, I'm gonna be all covered with it by the time I'm done here."

Tone finally lowered the bucket to me and climbed down the tree. There was nearly as much of the sticky goop all over him as there was in the bucket.

"Your mom's gonna have your head when she sees those jeans," I said.

"I'll hide them," he said, grinning.

"Let me go up next time," Willie begged.

The next one we found was practically on the ground. A fallen oak had broken down a jack pine, and there was a big gob of pitch right at the break. We scraped it off into the bucket and moved on through the woods.

"Look at that one," Tone said, tilting his head back and pointing up to pitch running down all around the broken top of a tall white pine.

"Guess it's my turn," I said. Following Tone's lead, I took off my shirt, tied the string from the bucket to my belt loop and began climbing to retrieve what appeared to be a mother lode. When I returned to earth, I, too, looked as though I had fallen into a tar pit. I was glad no one was waiting with a bucket of feathers.

"You're covered with it now, too," Tone said. "We're gonna need a bath in turpentine tonight."

"I want to do the next one," Willie pleaded.

"What is your mom gonna say if you get pitch all over your overalls, Willie?"

"Don't worry about that," he said grinning.

When we found the next pitch tree, Willie unhooked the straps on his bib shorts. They fell to the ground and he stepped out of them. In his underwear and with the bucket cord held tightly between his teeth, he climbed that tree like a monkey. Willie chipped off the pitch and in short order he was back on the ground. He was a sticky mess too, but at least his overalls were still clean. "See, don't worry about my clothes. I don't need 'em," he said grinning like a goof.

"Jeez, Willie, you're something else."

Farther into the woods we came upon a huge white pine that had been struck by lightning near the top. The upper one fourth of the tree was toppled over and just barely hanging on, and a huge amount of pitch had seeped from both the trunk and the broken top.

"Wow! There's enough up there to fill the rest of the buckets," I said. "Too bad this tree is so tall. I don't think we should try climbing up that high."

"I can climb it," Willie proclaimed.

"Willie, that's seventy feet up. Let's just let it go."

"I can climb it easy. Let me do it. I'm not scared."

32

I looked at Tone and he shrugged his shoulders. "You can try, but be careful. That's a long drop and I bet your Ma would be real pissed at us if we brought you home in the wagon, all busted up."

Willie grinned from ear to ear and tied the end of the light rope around his ankle. "Give me a boost up to those lower branches," he instructed us.

Tone laced his fingers together making a step for Willie, easily lifting him up as Willie grabbed the lowest branch and swung up onto it. Then he began his squirrel-like climb right up the side of the tree.

"Slow down, Willie, you're getting up there pretty high," I yelled up to him.

He paused for just a moment, looked down and nodded, and then continued the climb. In a very short time he was at the top. With his legs wrapped around a branch, he untied the line from his ankle and pulled up the bucket and chisel. It didn't take long for him to fill that bucket. He lowered it down on the rope, and we tied on another empty. Soon, a third bucket went up to Willie, and soon it was full of pitch, too.

"That's enough, Willie. Come back down before you fall and kill yourself."

"There's still a bucket full of pitch on the top of the tree yet. Tie on another bucket and I'll get that before I come down."

We tied on the last empty bucket and he pulled it up. Once he got the bucket, he tied it to a branch and climbed farther out on the limb to reach the broken top. As he got farther out on the branch, there came a cracking sound and the limb he was sitting on broke under his weight. Willie began falling through the branches and dropped a good ten feet before he managed to grab hold of one and stop his fall.

There he was, hanging from a rather small branch, and the next one beneath him just a little too far for his feet to reach.

"Willie! Jeez! Hold on. I'll come up and help you!" Tone shouted and ran to the tree. I made a handhold for him and boosted him up to the first branch, and he started up the tree.

33

"Hang on, Willie!"

"I'm hanging on, but hurry. This branch is pretty skinny!"

Tone made his way up the tree as fast as he could and when he got to where Willie was hanging, he stopped on a big branch and worked his way out on it as far as he dared.

"Willie, I'm gonna grab you around the waist. Then pull yourself toward me on that branch and let go."

Willie looked pretty scared but he nodded his head in acknowledgement of Tone's directions.

Tone crept out slowly on the next branch just below Willie. He reached up and got his arm around Willie's waist and hung on tightly to the branch next to him. "Okay Willie. Hand over hand toward me and let go."

Willie took a deep breath and obeyed Tone's instructions. He inched his way toward the tree trunk and Tone, and then finally let go of his grip on the branch. Tone pulled at the same time and Willie wrapped his arms around Tone's neck. Tone steadied himself on the branch, hoping it would hold the weight of both of them.

"Okay, Willie. Take hold of this branch above us and I'll move closer to the trunk. Tone moved in and Willie settled where Tone had been.

Willie grinned at Tone. "Good catch."

We all sighed with relief as Willie started down the tree. Tone untied the bucket, lowered it to me and then let the line drop. Then he followed Willie down the tree.

Willie hopped to the ground and watched Tone make his descent. When Tone swung down to the ground, Willie broke out in a big grin. "I guess I owe you one," he said as he stuck out his hand.

Tone shook Willie's hand and then locked his elbow around Willie's neck and ruffled his hair. "I'll keep that in mind, kid, next time I have some chores that need doing."

We toted our buckets of pitch back to the wagon and started for home. Mom was a little upset when she saw us and our jeans all covered with pitch. She ordered us out of the house. "Get to the barn and clean that stuff off with some turpentine," she scolded.

"Thanks for letting me help," Willie said when he had cleaned most of the pitch off himself. "And thanks for saving my neck, Tone," he added as he scampered off for home with his bib shorts thrown over his shoulder.

"See ya, Willie," Tone and I both said grinning. Tone shook his head. "What a nutty kid. But he sure is a lot of fun."

"I'll see you in the morning," Tone said as he began walking across the back yard to his house in his under shorts.

"Yeah, see you then," I said. I went into the house and Mom had a big pot of water heating for my bath.

"Don't touch anything! You smell like turpentine," Mom barked. "Just march right into the bathroom."

I didn't argue. I went straight to the bathroom and waited until Mom dumped the hot water into the tub. I added a second pail of cool water and got in. It took a lot of soap to get the turpentine smell off, but I finally managed. With a towel wrapped around myself, I went upstairs to get on some clean clothes.

"Come on down and get some supper," Mom called to me. "I saved some for you. And go tell Tone to come for supper, too. His mother is at work and your dads are out in the shop. I don't want him to have to eat alone."

I had to smile at Mom. She could act mad, but it didn't ever last long.

Tone was rummaging around in the kitchen in his shorts when I walked in. His hair was wet so I knew he had taken a bath, too, to get rid of the turpentine.

"Get some clothes on and come on over. Mom has supper for us."

"Is my dad over there?" he asked.

"Yeah," I said, nodding and grinning. "They're working on the boat."

Chapter 8

The day after our first tree sap excursion, Tone and I found a note from Mr. DeSilva pinned to the back screen door of my house. It said he needed us to dig a grave for old Mrs. Crowley as soon as possible. We changed into our work clothes and hurried over to the Funeral Home.

"Hi, boys," Mr. DeSilva greeted us. "Thanks for coming so quickly. We've got to get Mrs. Crowley buried as soon as possible."

"What's the rush?" Tone inquired.

"She died in bed three or four days ago and nobody noticed until this morning when she didn't show up for church. She's a little ripe and we need to get her in the ground."

"We can start right now," I said. "Is the grave marked?"

"Sure is. I put a stake on the spot and tied a ribbon to it. It's right by her late husband. Shouldn't be hard to find," Mr. DeSilva said.

Tone and I loaded the tools on Mr. DeSilva's wagon and drove down to the cemetery. We found the stake with the ribbon. "Well, let's get at it," Tone sighed. It was a rather warm day for grave digging.

We measured out the grave, cut the grass out and piled it to one side. Then we laid a canvas down and began shoveling the dirt onto it. While we dug we talked about what we needed by next spring for the cabin. Just as we were about half finished, Willie came running through the gravestones carrying a big jug of lemonade and some cups.

"Hi, guys. Mr. DeSilva told me you were here. I thought you'd be thirsty so I had my Ma make you some lemonade."

"Jeez, Willie. That was nice of you," I said as I climbed from the hole. Willie poured us each a cup of lemonade, and while we were taking a break, Willie climbed down into the hole and began digging.

"You don't have to do that," I said to Willie.

"I wanna help," he said.

Tone winked at me and said under his breath, "I think he's just happy to have somebody other than his sisters to hang around with. Let's let him help. He's a good kid." Good old Tone. He always looked out for the little guy.

After our little break, we took over the shoveling, and Willie took a break, and we began talking again about our cabin.

Tone started with his idea for some of the inside furnishings. "I was thinking we could build a bed frame with logs, and instead of a spring we could make a net with thin ropes that we could put a mattress on."

"That's a good idea," I said. "And we can build a table with some of our lumber... maybe a couple of stools... and a shelf to put stuff on."

Willie had already heard us talking about our island cabin and our plans for the next summer. "So you're gonna stay all summer on the island?" he asked.

"Yeah, that's the plan."

"Boy, that sounds like a fun time."

Tone and I went right on with our discussion. "We've got to find some dishes and pots and pans and blankets and maybe an old rug for the floor."

"It's too bad we don't have some way to keep food cold," Tone commented.

"I've been thinking about that," I said. "If we can find an island that's high enough over the water, we can dig a hole and put a big metal pail with a lid in the hole. The cool sand will be like an icebox. I think it'll work if we find the right island."

Willie was eager to be helpful again. "We've got an old metal pail with a tight lid in our shed," he said. "I bet my Ma will let you have it if you want."

"Great, Willie!" Tone grinned at his little buddy.

We soon had Mrs. Crowley's grave finished. "Wow, that seemed to go pretty fast," Tone said.

"Yeah, you're right. I guess talking about our cabin was a

good idea. It passed the time real fast."

"And Willie helped, too. That made it go faster," Tone said.

Willie grinned.

We packed up the shovels and other tools and drove the wagon back to the Funeral Home.

"We're done, Mr. DeSilva," I said as we stepped into the embalming room.

"Can you give Mrs. Crowley a lift into her box?" Mr. DeSilva called to us.

Tone looked at me and made an ugly face. "I guess so. Is she ready?"

"As ready as she's ever going to be," Mr. DeSilva replied.

Willie stopped dead in the doorway when he saw Mrs. Crowley on the slab. The smell was bad enough, but the sight of Mrs. Crowley lying there was about enough to make us all run for the door. Instead of being white and pasty, like we had seen other corpses, Mrs. Crowley was kind of a purplish black color.

"Oh boy. Let's get this over with," Tone groaned.

We stepped up to the table and tried not to look at the old naked lady laying there smelling up the place. We took hold of her and slid her into the casket, and then immediately headed for the door. Once we were outside we took a couple of deep breaths, and went over to the pump and washed our hands and threw a little cool water on our faces.

Willie stood there looking a little pale. "I never saw a naked lady before."

"Too bad that was the first one, Willie," Tone said. "That was pretty bad. Most naked ladies would be a lot better looking than that."

Mr. DeSilva came out smiling at us. "She's the first bad one you guys have had to move, isn't she?"

"Yes sir. I hope there aren't too many like that," I said.

"Thankfully, most aren't," he said as he handed us three dollars. "Here's for the grave and the help moving her. You guys came right away and did a good job, and I appreciate that."

"Thanks, Mr. DeSilva!" we both exclaimed. Three dollars! A lot of kids our age didn't see three dollars in a whole year.

Tone and I exchanged glances. We were experiencing one of those wordless communications that we often had. Tone handed one of the dollars to Willie. "Here, Willie. Here's your share."

Willie's mouth dropped open. "I can't take that. I didn't do hardly any work."

"You've helped us a lot lately. Go ahead. Take it." When Willie didn't take the money from Tone's hand, Tone tucked the dollar bill into the pocket on the front of Willie's bibs.

Willie took it out of his pocket and held the dollar out to Tone. He looked sad. Tears welled up in his eyes. "I don't want it. I just like it when we're friends. I don't want to be your hired helper."

Tone put his arm on Willie's shoulder. "Willie, you *are* our friend. We like it when you're with us, and when you help us, you deserve a share of the pay. Take the dollar and buy something nice for your Ma."

A tear trickled down Willie's cheek. He hugged Tone and then he hugged me. He put the dollar in his pocket and shuffled off toward his house.

I put my arm around Tone's shoulders and gave him a little squeeze. "That was a nice thing to do," I said.

"Willie's had some tough years. He needs something happy in his life. It was worth it... don't you think?"

I didn't have to ponder on that answer. "You bet I do."

We started walking toward home. "Well, we didn't get any boat pitch today," Tone said, "but we made a pile of money, and we made one little boy pretty happy." He seemed quite satisfied with the day's accomplishments, even though they had nothing to do with the boat progress.

"Yeah, there's always tomorrow for pitch," I replied. "And our dads won't be needing it for a while, anyway."

The weekend was coming up, and just in case the boat took shape faster than we expected, we'd be hauling pitch every day. And we could count on help from our new best friend, Willie.

Chapter 9

D ad and Robert were working on a house even though it was Saturday. They wanted to get everything closed in so they could continue the work during the cold weather. They wouldn't be working on the boat that day, so Tone and I decided to go on another pine pitch mission. Mom packed some sandwiches in an empty lard pail and put some apples and bananas in a bag. I filled a canteen with water. We were ready to make a day of it gathering pitch.

"We should ask Willie to come along," Tone suggested. He'll be disappointed if we don't."

We hitched Carl to the wagon so we could haul more than one pail of pitch back from the woods. Before we had even come to a stop in front of Willie's house, Willie ran across the front yard. "Hi guys! Need some help?"

"We're going out to the woods for more pitch, Willie. Feel like climbing trees again today?"

"You bet. I'll run in and tell Ma where I'm going." He ran into the house and we could hear him yelling to his mom: "I'm going to the woods with Tone and Ladd... I'll be back later." The door had hardly slammed shut and he was running across the yard again.

"Come and sit up here on the seat with us," I said. I slid over and made a space for him in the middle.

Willie jumped up and squeezed right in. His grin was nearly

as wide as the wagon.

Several trails on the high bank led to summer cottages along the river where the owners spent Sundays and holidays, and hunting and fishing trips, too. We found many trees along the trail with pitch runs, and we had soon collected three more pails of pitch than during our first outing.

"I wonder how much we'll need?" I pondered.

"I'd think this is enough," Tone concluded. "If it isn't, we can always get a little more."

This time we had a jar of turpentine and a bar of soap with us so we could clean up in the river, and we wouldn't get yelled at when we got home. The trail eventually led right down to the riverbank. We tied the horse to a scrub oak and walked along the river, just taking in the view. There was an island a little ways downstream that looked like it might be just right for our cabin.

About forty yards from shore with a nice, fast channel between, the island appeared to be about thirty feet wide and fifty feet long. The upper end was real high – six or seven feet above the water level, with a wide sandy beach at the lower end. It seemed just what we were looking for.

"Boy, that looks like the perfect island," Tone said. "Let's clean up here and swim over and take a look. Willie? Can you swim that far?"

"I swim like an otter. Wanna race?"

We took off our clothes, cleaned off the pitch with a rag soaked it in turpentine, and then waded into the river for a good, soapy bath.

"Whooie!" Tone said as he got in up to his waste. "That's the worst part – that one step where you get *it* wet."

"Whooie!" I said, laughing as I reached the same point.

Willie didn't wade in that far. When the water depth reached his thighs, he just dove in. He swam under water for several yards and then came up to the surface. "Yikes! That's a little brisk!"

Tone and I waded a little farther and then swam to the island.

As we neared the island, we dove down to see how deep the water was there. It was really deep.

"This is a good place for fishing," Tone said. "Plenty deep here."

Already on the island, Willie ran and shot himself off the bank, curling up like a cannonball, hitting the water right in front of us as we swam closer, nearly drowning us with the big splash. He giggled as he came to the surface and raced back to the sand.

Tone and I waded up onto the sand beach. It was perfect. We all strolled through the grass and trees to the island's upper end where we found a nice, level spot that would make a great place for our cabin.

"We can use a couple of these trees for corners," Tone said. "That'll make the cabin real sturdy."

"I'm gonna swim back and get our lunch pail," I said. "Let's have our lunch over here. Then we can swim and enjoy the day."

Tone thought that was a great idea.

"I'll go along and help you," Willie said, and he dove off the island into the river, swimming back to shore before I even had a chance to move.

"No shortage of enthusiasm," I said to Tone, laughing.

I swam back to shore to retrieve the lunch and the canteen. Willie grabbed the sack of fruit. With the canteen strap over my shoulder and the handle of the pail held between my teeth, I swam to the island on my back. Willie passed me half way. Tone lay in the sand watching and laughing.

"This is going to be a perfect place," Tone said. "I wish we didn't have to wait for winter and school to be over. I wish we could start our cabin right now."

"Yeah, me too, but then we'd have to leave it all winter. Better just wait and do it in the spring."

We ate our sandwiches, went for a swim, and then we all dozed off lying in the sun. We woke up a while later, not knowing how long we had been sleeping. "Boy! Your butt is really sunburned," Tone said.

Willie burst out laughing, "Ladd's got red buns."

"Yeow, that sun's hot! That's my Norwegian white skin," I whined. "I don't get that part of me in the sun very often." Tone's dark complexion wouldn't burn if he tried. "And Willie. How come you're not burned? You seem to be tan all over."

Willie grinned. "You know me – clothes and me don't agree when it's summer out."

We decided to swim back to shore and go home. All our clothes were right where we left them on the riverbank. After we got dressed and took the horse down to the river for a drink of water, we climbed onto the wagon and started for home. I sat carefully on my sunburned butt and each bump in the road made me wince. Willie thought it was hilarious. He sat between us on the wagon seat and chattered constantly all the way home.

Chapter 10

For the next couple of weeks, Dad and Robert worked on the boat whenever they had time. It seemed to be a pleasant diversion for them from their regular work routine. They went at it slowly, carefully inspecting each piece of wood for splits, knots, warping, how the grain ran, and any flaws that might affect how and where the board should be used. Trying to calm our impatience, they explained that many of the pieces had to be curved, and just the right piece of wood made a big difference in how well it all fit together. Carefully measuring and cutting each part, they gave it to Tone or me for sanding and planning until it fit just right. They cut mortise and tenon joints and vigilantly glued everything together. It all took time, and Tone and I did whatever we could to help, but much of the time that involved staying out of the way. We realized that if we had engaged this project on our own, our boat would have been a disaster, so we struggled to be patient.

Willie came over each evening, eager to be of help, too, and probably seeking an escape from his sisters' torment. We were really getting to like and admire the boy, and his intensions seemed purely from the heart. We couldn't say "no" when he asked if he could be there.

Our pile of boards slowly began taking the shape of a boat like we had never seen before. The deck was flat and wide and narrowed at the ends that gracefully curved upward. It curved up to form the sides that rose up in graceful arcs to the gunwale. Each end tapered to a point so it would cut through the water like a knife. The wide bottom gave it stability and would make it ride high so we could paddle it in very shallow water. At least that was the idea that Dad and Robert explained to us as we watched the boat take shape.

Once the main shell was finished, Dad cut trim pieces that finished off the gunwale, and Robert made ribs that attached across the bottom from side to side to give the boat stiffness and durability. Wedge shaped pieces of wood attached at the point on each end gave the boat more added strength and made little cubby holes to store things out of the rain. Finally, they built the two seats and installed them just far enough from each end so we could sit facing either direction and still paddle. There was really no front or back to the boat – each end was a mirror image of the other.

Dad fastened a clamp on the last seat brace; he stood back to admire the vessel he and Robert had created.

"Robert? I think we've missed our calling. We should have been boat builders."

"Well, maybe so," Robert replied. "It sure looks nice, but will it float?"

Tone and I looked at them questioningly and they both began laughing. "Got ya."

"Okay," Dad said. "Now comes your share of the work."

"We're ready! We've been ready to do something for almost a month," I said.

"Well, here's what you do," Dad said. "First, build a good fire in the stove and heat up a pail of water. Then put some of your pine pitch in a smaller pail and set it in the pail of hot water. The pitch will melt and when it turns to liquid, get all of the bark and dirt out of it with some old spoons. When it's clean, carefully pour pitch into each seam in the boat with a ladle, and make sure that every crack is filled, inside and out. Let it harden for a few hours and then the fun starts."

"Fun?" I questioned.

"Yeah, fun," he went on to explain. "With a sharp chisel, very carefully scrape off the excess pitch, and then sand the surface smooth. Do it in sections – pitch one area, let it dry, scrape it, sand it, and then move on to another area. Take your time, and do a good job. This is the most important part. If you mess it up, your boat will leak, and I guarantee – you won't like that."

Tone and I were eager to get to work. Dad and Robert left us to it. They had been working on the boat every hour they could spare for the last month. I think they were looking forward to a little rest.

Chapter 11

The next day after school Tone and I scrounged in his mom's cupboard for an old pot for melting the pitch. Tone finally came out with a pot with a broken handle that he had never seen his mom use, and it would be perfect for what we needed. We "borrowed" a slotted spoon and a ladle from her, too, and then Willie showed up with another big spoon.

We got a roaring fire going in the stove in Dad's shop and heated a pail of water. Some of the pitch went into the smaller pot, and the pot went into the hot water, just like Dad had instructed. Impatiently we waited for the pitch to start melting, but it didn't take long for the hard sap to look like golden syrup. We took turns stirring it and straining out the bark, dirt, and bugs with the slotted spoon. When it was all syrupy and clear, I wrapped a rag around the pot and carried it to the boat that rested on sawhorses. Tone dipped the ladle into the pitch and dribbled a stream of it into the middle seam on the bottom of the boat. He refilled the ladle and dribbled some into the next seam, and the next, until the pitch began to get stiff again.

"Better heat it up some more," I said, and set the pot back into the hot water.

Meanwhile Willie was chopping up the hard pitch into small pieces for the next batch that we would heat. We spent the rest of the evening heating and cleaning and pouring pitch into the cracks, and when we finally quit for the night, all the seams on the bottom of the boat were filled. The hardest work was yet to come.

The next day the pitch was rock hard. "Time to start scraping," Tone said.

Each with a wood chisel from Dad's tool cabinet, we began scraping off the excess hardened pitch. It wasn't easy, but it wasn't difficult, either. It just took patience and time. Tone and I scraped the sides and Willie climbed up into the boat and worked on the middle of the deck. That system seemed to work quite well.

We finished scraping the bottom that evening and the next evening we started sanding. It took a lot of elbow grease to make it all nice and smooth, but we worked hard and soon the bottom of our boat looked really good. We were all covered with a fine gray dust from the sanding. Willie's face was nearly white, but his smile told us that he was enjoying himself.

When the bottom was finished, we propped the boat up so we could work on the side while it lay flat. We went through the same procedure – heating, cleaning, pouring, scraping, and sanding – and in a couple of days that side was finished. Three more days and the other side was done. Then we turned the boat upside down and began working on the outside.

After two weeks of filling, scraping and sanding, we were glad to be done with the sealing job. It was a lot of hard work.

"Well, she looks pretty good," I said, as Tone and I wiped the dust from the hull with damp rags.

We turned the boat upside down with lighted lamps hanging above it. Willie slowly crawled along under it, looking for any light coming through a crack that we might have missed. After quite some time, he finally came out.

"She looks watertight, captain," he said saluting.

Tone and I laughed and I gave Willie a hardy pat on the back. "You're a nut, Willie. Do you know that?"

Willie just beamed a dazzling smile. "She's beautiful," he said. "Gonna paint it... or something... aren't we?"

"I guess we ought to ask our dad's what to do next."

Dad and Robert examined the boat with a careful eye. They even got under it just like Willie had done to see if there was any light coming through from above.

"It looks real tight," Dad said. "You guys did a good job."

"I could have told you that," Willie said.

"Now what do we do next?" Tone asked.

"Well," Robert thought a moment. "You can either paint it with some marine paint, or seal it with waterproof varnish."

48

"This boat is so good looking," Dad commented. "It would be a shame to cover all that nice wood with paint." After a moment or two of thought, he added, "Of course, the varnish is a lot more expensive."

"How much does the varnish cost?" I asked.

"Well, it's about seventy cents a quart, and it'll take four or five quarts to do a really good job. You should put on at least five or six coats," Dad said.

"So it would cost about three dollars?"

"Yeah, about that much. I know that's a lot of money," Dad said.

Tone looked my way and smiled. "Good old Mrs. Crowley," he chuckled.

I nodded. "We got paid three dollars to dig Mrs. Crowley's grave and move her stinky body from the slab to the box. And we have some other money saved up, too, so we've got plenty for the varnish."

"I want to donate that dollar you gave me for helping," Willie piped up.

"No, Willie. You keep your money," Tone said.

Willie's lower lip stuck out. "You gave it to me and you said I should do something nice with it. I want to buy you some varnish for the boat."

Tone and I exchanged glances and nodded to each other. "Well, Willie," I said. "Only if we make you a one third partner."

"Really? No foolin'?"

"No foolin,' Willie. You've helped us from the very start. She's now one third yours."

Dad and Robert laughed. "Well, you guys have that all worked out. But I can't say that I'd want to trade jobs with you... moving dead bodies and digging graves," Robert said. "But this boat ought to give you a lot of enjoyment for your labors."

"We've got a bunch saved up," Tone said. "Next summer is going to be one to remember. If people keep dying at a good rate, we'll be rich."

"Are you going to name the boat?" Dad asked.

"Yeah, I guess we should."

"I know just the name," Tone said. "Remember when we read about Father Marquette? They called them the Voyageurs. How about that for a name?"

I thought about it for a moment. "That's perfect," I said.

"How about I carve it into each side?" Willie said, digging his trusty jack knife from a pocket. "I'm a real good carver."

Tone and I agreed. "Have at it Willie."

Dad found some carving chisels for Willie, and he and Robert left. Willie carefully measured the center of each side, and then sat down on the floor and slowly began carving, his tongue sticking out the corner of his mouth as he concentrated on his work. Tone and I sat and watched as he expertly carved the name into the side of the boat:

Voyageur

Chapter 12

After Willie carved the name, *Voyageur,* into each side of the boat, he carefully stained the lettering with some dark wood stain that Dad had for some cabinets he was building. It looked fantastic.

We gave Dad the money and he bought just the right varnish for us at the hardware store. Then for the next couple of weeks we varnished the boat. We'd paint a coat on with brushes and let it dry overnight. The next day we'd sand the previous day's work with fine sandpaper until it was perfectly smooth and wipe it down with a damp cloth.

Then we'd turn the boat over and do the inside the same way. We went back and forth from the inside to the outside and had applied seven coats on each side before we ran out of varnish. Each coat gave the boat a darker, golden honey colored luster, and made it more and more beautiful.

"I'd bet there isn't another boat as good looking as this one anywhere on the Wisconsin River," Willie bragged as he stepped back and admired our sleek, golden craft. "I doubt if there's a prettier boat in the whole world."

That evening, Tone's mom wasn't working, so we all went to

his house for supper. She made a huge dish of ravioli and a big basket of garlic bread, and we even had some wine. That was a real treat for Tone and me. Of course, Willie had to settle for apple juice.

With our two families laughing and enjoying each other's company, Tone and I felt very rich, indeed. We were lucky to have such great parents and to be able to share them the way we did. And now, we were glad to share them with Willie, too. He was becoming more like a little brother to us.

"We'll clean up and wash the dishes," I said, and Tone and Willie nodded. "Sit on the porch and have some more wine, and after we've finished, we want to show you the boat." Our moms protested, insisting that they'd do the dishes, but our dads convinced them to relax and to let us take care of the cleanup. "Our sons are turning into young men," Dad said.

Willie started to clear the table while Tone and I began washing plates. Both moms smiled and gave each of us a kiss on the cheek. They hugged Willie and kissed him, too. "And this one is such a sweetie," my mom said. "I think I'll keep him."

Willie beamed a big, toothy grin.

Then Tone's mom added, "We're lucky to have such good boys." Directing her focus on Willie, she said, "And one of these days you're going to make all the girls crazy as loons."

That thought put a horrified expression on Willie's face. "Ack! Girls are icky!"

I grinned at Tone, "He won't think that way in a few more years."

Willie stuck his finger in his throat and pretended to throw up.

After we finished the dishes, we led the moms and dads to the shop. As Willie and I ushered them in, Tone ran ahead to light some lanterns. When the light brightened, there sat our boat for all to see. Its shiny finish nearly sparkled under the lamplight.

"My goodness! It's beautiful," Tone's mom said. "I never imagined it would be so sleek and pretty. It's almost like the gondolas in Venice."

"It's wonderful boys," Mom said, her eyes getting wet. "Just wonderful."

Our dads smiled. They were proud of their construction, and I'm sure they were pleased with our care in finishing the job.

"We couldn't have done it without our dads," I said, as Tone and I both hugged them.

On the way out Angela recognized her slotted spoon and ladle. "I wondered where that went."

"We'll get you some new ones, Mom," Tone said.

She put her arms around our shoulders and began walking us back to the house. "Don't worry about it. I've got lots of others. I'm just glad you put them to good use. I thought I was getting forgetful and couldn't remember where I put them."

"You're not *that* old, Mom," Tone said.

The evening was becoming chilly as fall came a little closer each day. It would be a long time to wait to use the boat, but when the time came, we'd be ready.

Chapter 13

The days were getting shorter and cooler. Fall was definitely in the air. Tone and I were back in school, studying hard and looking forward to our birthdays that weren't far off.

Our savings had grown with the deaths of three more citizens, so we were flush with money again. Tone and I were in his bedroom studying one late afternoon when we noticed Mr. DeSilva knocking on the door at my house. We grabbed our jackets and ran across the yard to see what he wanted.

"Hi, Mr. DeSilva," we said as we came around the corner. "Need a hole dug?" Tone asked.

"Hi, boys. No, not today. But I could use your help for a couple of hours."

"What's up? Is there a body to move?" I asked.

"No, not that either," he said, shaking his head. "Remember Mr. Honer? He's here with my fall load of caskets. We'd like you boys to unload them. Business has been good and I had to order some more, to make sure I have enough over the winter."

"We'd be happy to, Mr. DeSilva," Tone said.

We jumped on the back of Mr. DeSilva's wagon and rode with him to the Funeral Home. There sat Mr. Honer on the seat of his big wagon. He gave us a hearty wave when he saw us. "There are my young lads. How are you fellows? And where's that young Willie today?"

"We're great, Mr. Honer, and I suppose Willie is at home, but he'll probably be here pretty quickly when he sees us over here working. You two just go on up to the hotel and take a little break. We'll take care of the unloading. We know exactly what to do."

Mr. Honer grinned and said to Mr. DeSilva, "If these lads ever need a permanent job, let me know. I'd hire them at my factory in a minute."

Mr. Honer boarded Mr. DeSilva's wagon and they drove off up

the street to the hotel. Tone and I began unloading the caskets and it was only a few minutes later when Willie came trotting into the driveway. "Need some help?"

Willie had finally given in to the colder weather. He was wearing a shirt and shoes with his bib overall shorts.

"Willie? When are you going to start wearing long pants and socks again?"

He laughed. "There's no snow yet. No need for them, is there?"

Tone and I chuckled. "Too bad you don't live in Hawaii. You'd fit right in like a native."

We unpacked the fancy caskets from their crates, and after Willie had dusted them off, they were put in their proper places. All the packing straw and the smashed crates were on fire, and as the fire was burning down, the two men came riding down the street in the wagon.

"Done already?" Mr. Honer said. "Ah, young Willie, how are you, lad?"

"I'm good, Mr. Honer. How's yourself?"

"Couldn't be better, Willie," he said shrouding Willie's shoulders with a comforting arm. "So you lads don't need the crates this time for your project?"

"No sir. Our boat is all finished," Tone said.

"And how did your boat turn out?" Mr. Honer asked.

"Before you leave town, drive over there with the boys and see that boat," the undertaker said. "You'll not believe it."

Mr. DeSilva paid us a dollar and Mr. Honer offered to give us a ride home so he could see the boat. We parked his team and wagon in the street and walked around the house back to Dad's shop. When we opened the shop doors, our boat glistened in the afternoon sunlight.

"There she is. What do you think?" Tone said.

Mr. Honer just stood there with his mouth hanging open. He stepped up closer and slid his hands along the sleek sides of the boat, looking it over carefully.

"I'm speechless, boys. You made this from those old crates?"

"Yes, sir."

"This is a work of art. It's a thing of beauty." He saw *Voyageur* carved into the wood. "And who did this wonderful carving?"

"Willie did that. He helped us with the whole boat, too."

"We helped, but our dads actually built it," I explained. "We did the finishing, though – all the sealing and sanding and varnishing."

"This is as fine workmanship as I've ever seen." Mr. Honer seemed quite impressed. "Your fathers should be casket makers. They're artists. And the finish, too, is as fine as any I've seen."

We were basking in the compliments when Dad and Robert drove into the yard. They started to unload some tools from Dad's wagon.

"Dad? Robert? This is Mr. Honer – the man who builds caskets for Mr. DeSilva. He was just admiring your work."

Mr. Honer stuck his hand out to shake with them. "Call me Harvey. You fellas are artists. That's a fine piece of work. I'm very impressed."

"Robert designed it and we worked on it together," Dad said. "The boys did all the finish work."

"So they told me. It's a fine boat, indeed! Maybe the finest I've ever seen."

"It's kind an early birthday present for our boys. They turn sixteen next week," Robert said.

"Both in the same week?" Mr. Honer asked.

"Yes, they're only two days apart, but we celebrate their birthdays on the day in between... on the 15th," Dad said.

"Well, that's a wonderful thing. Two families that are so close. And two boys that are such good friends. And taking this fine young lad for a friend, too," he said putting his hand on Willie's shoulder. "I've no family myself. The wife passed away nearly ten years ago, and my son was lost in a fire when he was only thirteen. So I just spend my time working. You are truly a blessed group of people to have such a fine family life," he praised.

Tone and I shook hands with Mr. Honer. "You're always welcome here, sir. We're glad to know you, and we're here whenever you need help with your caskets."

"And anytime you need a boy to talk to, let me know, Mr. Honer. I think you're a pretty good guy," Willie said, giving him a broad smile.

Mr. Honer returned a pleasant smile to us all, and to Willie in particular. "That's a great thing to know, young Willie. It truly is. Well, I had better be heading north. It's a long haul back to Wausau – takes me nearly a week to get home, so I'd better get started."

We walked with him to the street and he climbed onto his wagon. As he slapped the horses with the reins he said, "See you boys next summer. Probably about the middle of July. Maybe we can take a boat ride together." And off he went.

Willie's sad smile watched Harvey drive down the street. "He sure is a nice man. Too bad he lost his family. I bet he'd be a good Pa."

Chapter 14

It always seemed that Tone and I had plenty of help to celebrate our birthdays, and this one, being our sixteenth, was nothing short of spectacular. Besides our parents and grandparents, several of Tone's mom's friends from work, our employer, Mr. DeSilva, and Willie and his mom and four sisters were there celebrating with us. It was quite a diverse group of people: Italians shouting and toasting with their bottles of Italian wine, and Norwegians laughing and enjoying their beer and some good Norwegian Aquavit. That's a strong liquor that has to travel across the equator and back in the hold of a sailing ship – so they say – before it is declared *real* Aquavit. .

And because of the difference in our heritage, our birthday feasts always featured an unusual combination of food characteristic of our nationalities. My family favored the Norwegian codfish, crumbcakka, lefse, and rommegrat, and the Trinchis liked their Italian spaghetti, rigatoni and garlic bread. All the others, if they weren't Italian or Norwegian, sampled some of each. Willie's mom baked a huge birthday cake with thirty-two candles on it.

Mr. DeSilva played his accordion and there was much singing and laughing. Since we had such a large group we cleaned up Dad's shop and held the party there. Our moms and grandmas had decorated it all in ribbons and balloons.

After everyone had eaten, Tone and I began to open our presents. We got our usual assortment of socks and underwear and shirts, which meant that we both had a lot of new clothes because we always traded them back and forth. Dad and Robert gave each of us a Swiss Army knife with all the different tools and gadgets. "They'll come in handy when you're out on the river next summer," Dad said.

"Dad, you didn't have to get us anything," I told him. "The boat is present enough for the rest of our lives."

But he just shrugged his shoulders and waved a hand as if it were no big deal.

Mr. DeSilva walked out to his buggy and brought in two large packages. "Boys, these are for you, and I want to tell you here in front of your relatives that I'm very glad I asked you to work for me last year. You're good boys and the best helpers I ever had. And, I'm real glad that we've worked out arrangements for next summer. I sure hated the idea of hiring some new helpers."

He had fretted and stewed for the last month about us being out on the river that next summer. But we had talked it over with him and we decided that since our boat had turned out so well, he could send a messenger who knew where to find us, and we could easily paddle up the river to town whenever he needed us. That made Mr. DeSilva really happy, and we were glad to be able to keep on making some money.

We opened the big boxes and inside each of them was what appeared to be a big fishing net. Looking quite perplexed, neither of us could figure out just what we had.

"They're hammocks," Mr. DeSilva informed. "All you do is string them between two trees or posts and you can sleep in them. I thought they'd be just the thing for your cabin."

"Wow! Thanks, Mr. DeSilva," we both said in unison.

We hadn't thought of hammocks, but they would work just great. On warm nights we could even sleep outside under the stars if we took a notion. And, when we weren't using them, we could roll them up and have more room in the cabin.

Just as we were inspecting the hammocks, a man from the freight office came to the door. "I've got a big package here for Tone and Ladd," he said. We had no idea who would have sent us a package. Everyone we knew was already at the party.

We walked with the deliveryman out to his wagon. He lifted out a long, thin box. "This is from someone named Honer," he said. "All you have to do is sign for it."

Tone signed the receipt and we toted the big, long box into the shop.

"My goodness, what could that be?" Mom said.

I found a pry bar and Tone and I began to open the crate. Under a bunch of packing material lay two of the most beautiful canoe paddles we'd ever seen, made of laminated strips of different colored wood. They were light and delicate but you could tell that they would be strong enough for the heaviest current.

There was a note tied to them:

Happy Birthday Tone and Ladd. I hope these get to you in time for your birthdays. They are the finest I could find and I think they'll look good with your beautiful boat. Enjoy many hours of paddling.

Your Friend,
Harvey Honer

We certainly hadn't expected to get a present from Mr. Honer, but it certainly was a most pleasant surprise.

"Wow. We sure got a lot of great stuff for our birthday," I said. Then Tone and I spent the next ten minutes making the rounds with Thank you hugs for everyone.

Everyone began talking and eating again and Mr. DeSilva played another lively tune on his accordion. We thought we were done with all the presents until Willie handed us each a small package.

"This is prob'ly not such a good present," he said shyly. "But you guys are always so nice to me, and I wanted to get you something."

We opened the packages. They each contained a St. Christopher medal hanging from a leather thong.

"In case you guys get lost or something," Willie said. "Ma says that St. Christopher is the Patron Saint of Travelers."

Tone squatted down, put his arms around Willie and hugged him tightly. "I'll wear it forever, and I'll think of you every time I look at it, my friend."

I hugged Willie, too, and whispered, "It's the best gift of all,

Willie, because it came from your heart. I'll always cherish it. Thanks."

Willie swallowed hard and blinked back a tear. "I wouldn't want anything to happen to my two big brothers," he said.

Tone and I tied the leather thongs around our necks and the medals hung on our chests. What a great birthday. We were slowly accumulating everything we would need for our summer on the river. We had just about everything figured out – everything, that is, except how to get that stove onto the island. That was a problem we might need some help solving.

Chapter 15

Winter 1913

The river had frozen over nearly two weeks earlier and the ground was white with snow. Outside the wind howled and more snow was falling. Tone and I were studying at his mom's kitchen table where the fire in the stove kept the room warm and toasty.

"Have you guys thought about how you're going to get your stove and lumber out to your island?" Tone's dad asked as he walked into the room.

"We can carry the wood across in the boat," I said, "but the stove is too heavy, so we're not sure about that."

"Any ideas, Dad?" Tone said looking up expectantly.

A sly smile slithered into Robert's expression. "I just might have one," he said. "I'm going to talk to Eric. We'll let you know if we come up with something."

Robert put on his coat, hat and boots and walked the path we had shoveled through the snow to my house. A while later, Tone noticed that our dads were going to the barn. "Let's go see what they're doing," he said eagerly.

We put on our coats and waded through the new snow to the barn where we found our dads inside with lighted lanterns, sorting through the tin roofing from the old summer kitchen.

"What are you looking for?" I asked.

"We're thinking that we can make a sled with some of this roofing tin and some beams from the summer house. We can strap the stove onto it and slide it out across the ice. One of the horses can pull it easy."

"Holy Toledo! Do you think it would work?"

"I don't see why not, as long as the ice is thick enough," Dad said. "Where's the island that you've decided on?"

We explained how to find our island by following the sand trail along the high bank. "It's about forty or fifty yards from the shore, but the water is deep and the current is pretty fast."

"Doesn't matter how deep it is as long as the ice is thick enough on top. Tomorrow's Saturday and we're not going to work. We'll go down there and take a look at it," Tone's dad said.

We could hardly wait for morning. We knew Willie would be disappointed if we went without him. We told him to come over first thing after breakfast so he could go with us.

Tone and Robert came over the next morning for breakfast. Just as we sat down, Willie came in, stomping the snow off his boots onto the rug by the door. "Holy smokes! The snow's a foot deep!" he said.

"Have you had breakfast, sweetie?" Mom asked.

"I didn't want to be late, so I just skipped it."

"Well, then, sit down and have some breakfast," Mom said, smiling at Willie. "Growing boys must eat."

He returned the smile with a big grin, shucked off his coat and boots, pulled up a chair and dug into the plate of eggs and toast.

"Nothing wrong with that boy's appetite," Dad said. "Willie, how do you stay so slim?"

"I'm just like a shrew," Willie said grinning. "I burn food as fast as I can eat it."

The snow had stopped falling during the night and the whole world looked like a picture postcard that someone would send for Christmas. We hitched up Carl and Jack, and the five of us piled into the cutter and took off for the river bottoms. The snow wasn't so deep, and the horses got along quite easily. It only took half an hour to get to the riverbank.

"That's it," I said pointing out across the ice to the island. "It's high enough that it shouldn't flood, and there are trees for firewood and shelter. And there's a nice sandy beach at the lower end for swimming and fishing."

"It looks like a good spot," Dad said.

Robert grabbed an ax, walked out onto the ice a short way and began chopping a hole. It took him many whacks with the ax to finally get to water. He knelt down and measured the ice. "There's a good ten inches here."

We walked about half way to the island and Robert chopped another hole. There was still ten inches of ice or more. "No problem with the ice," Dad said. "That much ice will easily hold up the horses and the stove."

Tone and I looked at each other with excited grins. Now all we needed was a sled strong enough to haul the stove. We all piled back on the cutter and rode back to town. Our cabin was becoming more of a reality every day.

Chapter 16

Robert and Dad built the sled in just two evenings with a sheet of our roof steel, four-by-fours, and two-by-six runners. They bent the front of the steel upward so it would go through the snow easier, and attached a stout beam that the horses could be hitched to. Tone and I were anxious all week for Saturday to arrive when we would take the stove across to the island.

Even though he couldn't lift much weight, Willie begged to help us. We maneuvered the sled into the doorway of the barn, and the five of us managed to get the stove moved onto it. Dad and Robert tied it down securely, harnessed Carl and hitched him to the sled. Dad would sit on the stove and drive Carl and the sled, and the rest of us would follow Dad to the river on the cutter hitched to Jack.

The sled pulled along real nice and it didn't take long to get to the riverbank. Our next problem was to get the sled and stove over the bank and onto the ice. Not far from the end of the trail, there was a low spot where the bank wasn't very steep. We positioned Carl and the sled near it, and tied two long ropes to the stove, stringing the ropes around a couple of stout trees to help hold back the sled as it went down the embankment, and to keep it from running over Carl.

Tone had a way with Carl, talking low and stroking his muzzle, coaxing him down the bank. The rest of us held the ropes, keeping the sled from going down faster than Carl was willing to. Carl was quite skittish, at first, about walking on the ice, but Tone finally sweet-talked him into stepping out onto it.

We managed to hold the sled from running into Carl, but as it started over the bank, it picked up a little speed, and made a sudden lunge onto the ice. Willie had all eighty of his pounds braced against the rope, but when the stove slid over the bank he went flying into the brush. He crawled out of the bushes with a wide grin on his face.

We all had to chuckle just a little.

"Okay," Robert called to Tone. "Start him across, nice and slow."

Carl was rather nervous, but he trusted Tone's lead as he pulled the sled easily across the frozen channel. He seemed a little calmer when he walked up onto the frozen sand on the lower end of the island. "Whoa Carl," Tone said, and patted the horse gently on his head. "Good boy, Carl." Brush and trees prevented Carl from going any farther.

"Okay," Dad said. "Let's see if we can get this thing off the sled and up to the other end of the island."

We untied the stove and slid it off the sled and onto the frozen, snow-covered ground. Willie stayed behind and held Carl while the rest of us carried the stove toward the high end of the island. It was heavy, clumsy, and hard to manage in the snow. When we had gone a ways, Dad called for a break. "No need to rush," he said.

We rested a minute and then lifted it again and carried it another several feet, took another rest, and carried again. When we finally got it to the high end of the island, we set the stove down and looked for the right spot to put it.

"Figured we'd use a couple of trees for corners," Tone said.

"Good idea," Robert responded. "And then you only have to dig in two other corner posts. That'll make your cabin real strong."

We found two trees about fifteen feet apart that would make good opposite corners. "If we dig in a post here and here," I said, pointing to the other two imaginary corners, "the stove will sit right about here." Everyone seemed to agree, and so we carried the stove to that spot and set it down in the snow.

Tone's imagination was at work. "I can see it already," he said with one of those far-away looks in his eyes. For just a moment, I could see it, too, and I nodded my head in agreement.

"One of you get that tarp from the cutter," Dad instructed. "We'll cover the stove so it doesn't get all rusty."

I retrieved the tarp and we tied it tightly over the stove. Then we all walked back from the island as Tone led Carl across the ice to the riverbank.

"We can haul the lumber if you guys don't want to come back," I said to Dad and Robert.

Dad drove the sled back behind Carl, and on the way home, Tone and I huddled together in the cutter, secretively discussing an idea that I had. Tone agreed with my suggestion, and when we got back to the barn, he dashed off to their house and got four dollars from our savings that was stashed in his bedroom.

"Take our moms out for supper tonight – on us," we said, handing the money to our dads.

"You guys don't have to do that. We're glad to help," Robert said.

But we insisted. "Take it, and give the moms a night off from cooking... and have fun! Without your help we wouldn't have a boat, and our stove wouldn't be delivered safe and sound." I said.

"Well, thank you, boys." They gave us each a loving pat on the back, and off we went to the barn to load some of the lumber onto the sled.

Willie was unusually quiet all during the three trips it took to get all the lumber hauled out to the river and carried across to the island. When we finished, we covered it and left it until spring.

Carl pulled us home on the sled and we arrived at the barn just as our moms and dads were leaving for their night on the town. Mom hadn't forgotten us, though. "There's chicken and all the fixin's in the oven," she called out to us. "And thanks for the dinner up town."

Then Tone's mom added, "Tone, why don't you sleep over in case we get home late." She and my mom laughed wickedly.

"Should we wait up for you?" We returned a wicked grin.

They all just laughed and started down the street.

Remembering that Willie had seemed a little down in the dumps, I turned to him. "Willie, why don't you run home and ask your mom if you can come for supper and then stay over with us. We'll have the house to ourselves."

"Are you sure it's ok?" he asked. A bit of a smile crept onto his face.

"Of course it's okay," I told him. "Unless you think you'll be homesick for your sisters."

Willie clutched his heart and acted like he'd been shot. "Gawd! Don't say stuff like that," he whined. Then a full-fledged smile came back. "I'll bring a deck of cards, too. I'm a pretty good poker player. You guys got any money left?"

Chapter 17

Spring 1914

Our last day of eleventh grade was almost upon us – final examinations on Monday and Tuesday, and we were finished for the summer!

Tone and I were progressively getting more excited about our upcoming adventure on the river. We had some of our savings with us and we were on our way to do some shopping. We would find a lot of the things we'd need in our cabin at the Second Hand store in town. Of course, we invited Willie along to help. He had become a permanent fixture at one or the other of our houses lately. He was a funny kid and we just enjoyed having him with us.

We had made a list and were poking around looking for the best bargains. "If you boys don't care about matching plates and glasses," Mr. Miller, the owner told us, "I can give you a good deal on stuff that I've only got one or two pieces."

"We really don't care if it matches," I said. "I don't think we're going to have any tea parties." Tone and I laughed. Willie made a pretend motion of holding a teacup daintily in his fingers with his pinky held up like some sophisticated lady, but he didn't look very ladylike in his bib overalls and bare feet.

We began choosing items and piling them on the counter. We needed a coffee pot, a kettle for heating water, pots and pans, utensils, silverware, and a couple of oil lamps. We found a small mirror, some sharp knives for cleaning fish, several blankets and three pillows. We'd take our baths in the river, but we picked out a basin and pitcher for washing and brushing our teeth in the mornings.

"Do you have any old rugs?" I asked the storekeeper.

"How big?"

"Well," Tone began. "Our cabin is going to be about ten or twelve feet square. We need something to keep from getting sand all over everything."

Mr. Miller rummaged around a bit in the back room and soon came out with a rolled up rug. "This is about twelve feet square, so it should be just about right. It's pretty worn, so you can have it for twenty five cents."

"Perfect. Now how about some towels?" Tone said.

We found just what we needed, paid Mr. Miller, and loaded our gear into the wagon.

"How come you got three pillows?" Willie asked as we left the store.

"Never know when you might need an extra pillow," I said. I winked at Tone.

"What are you guys winking about?"

"Just wait and see, Willie."

We went to the hardware store next, and bought a hundred feet of rope, two gallons of lamp oil, a pail for hauling water, two boxes of stick matches, some extra wicks for our lamps, and a few clothespins.

Mr. Marcus' market was our last stop. There we bought all of our basic groceries like salt, pepper, cooking oil, popcorn, and flour. We checked our list and everything was accounted for. "Well, I think we've got it all," I declared.

"We'll probably have to come back for something once we get settled in, but it looks good," Tone agreed.

We stored all of our supplies in the barn, and then went to our rooms to pack some clothes.

When Tuesday finally came and we finished our last hours of school, we were more than ready to begin our summer adventure. Our plan was to haul the boat to the river the next morning, paddle across to the island and begin work on the cabin. We'd sleep at home for a couple more nights, and then we'd be off on our great adventure! We could hardly wait for morning.

Chapter 18

I was just sitting down to breakfast when Willie tapped on the door. He had begged to come along to help with the cabin, and now he was showing up an hour early.

"Come on in, sweetie," Mom said when she saw him at the door. "Had your breakfast yet?"

"No, ma'am. I didn't take time for breakfast," he said.

"Well, sit yourself down and I'll make you something."

"So Willie," I said, grinning. "I see you're wearing your summer uniform." He had on his former school bib overalls that were now cut off shorts, was shirtless and barefoot. This is how we would see him dressed for the rest of the summer.

"Yup," he said with an impish grin. "No sense in wearing too many clothes in the summertime." If the truth were told, I think Willie would run around naked all summer if he thought he could get away with it.

Tone walked in just as we finished our breakfast. "Morning, Mom," he said, giving my mother a peck on the cheek.

"Good morning, number two son." She smiled warmly. "I guess I'll have to start calling Willie number three son."

Willie beamed.

We loaded the lunch that Mom packed for us, a water canteen, the tools Dad loaned us, several cans of nails, and our beautiful boat into the wagon and we were off to our first day of work on our island cabin. We could hardly wait for Carl to pull us to the riverbank. When we arrived, we unharnessed Carl and tied him to a tree in the shade where he could graze on the spring grass and get a drink from the river if he got thirsty.

The anticipation was overwhelming as we slid *Voyageur* over the bank to the water. We loaded it with the lunch and the tools and cans of nails, and then we stepped into our boat for the first time.

Tone took the front seat, I took the back seat, and Willie sat on the floor in the middle. We pushed away from the bank. The boat slipped out into the river like a swan swimming across a pond. We began paddling and *Voyageur* slid effortlessly through the water. "This handles like a dream," Tone said.

"No kidding! It hardly takes any effort to paddle," I said. "Our dads *should* have been boat builders."

We paddled across the channel to the island and beached the boat on the lower end in the sand. We got out and pulled the boat up so it wouldn't float away, and unloaded our tools. We walked to the upper end of the island, cutting a branch off here and there to clear our path. We'd be using this path hundreds of times, so it needed to be cleared. Once we got to the high end of the island, we found the stove and lumber, undisturbed. We checked out our cabin site, now that it was not covered with snow. It was just the way we remembered seeing it last fall.

Our first choice of the two trees to use for opposite corners was perfect. Both were soft maples, about twelve inches around and almost perfectly straight. After Tone scratched the outline of the floor in the sand, there were only a few bushes, small saplings, and one other larger tree that needed to be cleared away. Willie began chopping at them right away.

We cleared out the brush around the area and cut all of the branches off of the two corner trees up as far as we could reach. We cut off the other tree that would have been inside the cabin about three feet from the ground. If things worked out as planned, it would become part of our kitchen table. Then we went to our lumber pile to find two four-by-four corner posts.

We carefully measured where the posts should be buried, and we even made a diagonal measurement to ensure the cabin would be square. Then the three of us took turns digging, and buried the bottom three feet of each post in the sand. We decided where to put our door, measured for the opening, and soon had another post buried for that.

Then it was time to start cutting planks for the walls. We worked non-stop as the sun climbed to its peak and the cool morning air turned hot and muggy.

"Whew! It's getting hot and I'm getting hungry," Tone said.

"Yeah, me too. Let's take a break for some lunch."

We walked back to the boat to get the lunch and the canteen of water. We sat on *our* beach to eat our first meal on the island. Tone and I took off our shirts and shoes and enjoyed the sunshine while we ate our sandwiches.

"I think maybe a little nap might be okay, too," I suggested. Tone nodded his head and closed his eyes, and in less than a minute he was snoring softly. Willie lay on his back, slipped out of his bibs and fell asleep in his underwear.

It didn't take long for me to fall asleep, too, and an hour or so later I woke because of the cold water dripping on my face. Tone was standing over me dribbling water from the edge of a canoe paddle.

"Hey! Stop that!" I yelled.

Willie was awake, too, and was giggling at the joke Tone had pulled on me with the water. I jumped up and tackled Tone. We both ended up in the river, laughing and trying to dunk each other for several minutes. Then there was a big splash as Willie jumped into the water, climbed on my back and tried to take me under. I turned over on my back and put *him* under water until he ran out of breath. He finally let go and came up sputtering. "Jeez. You're trying to drown me."

He jumped on Tone and they wrestled around for a while, and then we all waded out of the water, winded.

"Well, I'm cooled off now," I said.

"Let's get back to work," Tone commanded, starting up the beach toward the cabin.

We finished the day working in our wet jeans. Willie slipped off his wet underwear and put on his dry shorts. Tone and I should have thought of that before we launched ourselves into the river.

We began cutting and nailing on planks for the walls. When we got up too high to reach, Willie sat on Tone's shoulders and hammered the nails, while I held the other end of each board.

The sun was getting low in the west when we decided to call it quits for the day. We had three of the walls finished. The only one left was where the window would be. Our next job would be to frame in a hole for the window in the back wall, and with any luck we'd finish the walls the next day, and maybe get started on the roof.

We stepped back to admire our creation. Tone put one arm across Willie's shoulders and the other across mine. "Well, my friends," he said proudly. "That's home for the next couple of months."

The corners of Willie's mouth drooped down and the sadness oozed out. "I bet you guys will have lots of fun out here."

Tone and I exchanged glances. "Maybe we should tell him," I said.

"Might as well," Tone agreed.

For the past several weeks, we had talked about asking Willie to stay with us at the cabin. We enjoyed his company, and he always seemed so happy to be with us. We thought it would be a good idea to invite him.

"Tell me what?" Willie asked.

"The *three* of us are spending the summer here, Willie. We want you to come and live with us in the cabin."

Willie's mouth dropped open. "You wouldn't be foolin' with me, would you?"

"No foolin,' Willie. We want you to stay with us. That's *if* you want to stay."

Willie did a back flip from a standing start. He landed on his feet, took off running down the island to the sand beach and jumped right into the river. I looked at Tone and he was grinning at Willie.

"I guess we can take that as a 'yes.'"

Chapter 19

We decided that moving our stove into place before we built the back wall would be the first job to get done on our second day. It was going to be hard enough to move without guiding it through a door, too. We only had to move it about ten feet, so after we got Carl all settled, we took the boat across and went right to work. Our guess at where to place it had been a little off with the snow covering everything last winter.

"Let's see if we can move it at all, first," I said.

Tone got on one side and I got on the other. Willie got in the middle and we lifted and slid at the same time. The stove moved about two inches.

"At this rate we'll have it inside the cabin by August," Tone said. "We need some way to slide it."

I had a sudden brainstorm. I went to the lumber pile and got two planks. I smoothed out two shallow trenches for the planks in the sand right in front of the two legs of the stove that were closest to the cabin. "Let's slide it onto these planks and see if it will move any easier."

When we tried to lift the front legs of the stove onto the planks, they slid out from under it, so we put them down again and Willie stood on them to keep them from moving. We managed to get the legs onto the planks, and then got behind the stove and pushed and lifted and slid it farther up onto the planks. Once it was on the smooth boards it slid along much easier. Willie got two more planks and put them at the ends of the first two. We slid the stove across the first planks and onto the second ones, and then moved the first planks to the front of the second ones. It only took ten minutes to get the stove to the cabin using the planks, and our heads.

"Not bad," Tone said. "Sometimes you come up with a pretty good idea, if I must say so."

"Thanks Tone. And you may say so," I said, grinning.

With the stove finally in its proper place, we began working on the back wall. In just a short time we had it up and the window installed in the hole we left for it.

Everything was looking good. The front wall was about one foot higher than the back, just as we had planned. The tops of the sidewalls were slanted so the roof would be pitched downward toward the back of the cabin. Then all the rain would run off the back of the roof. We boosted Willie up on the roof and he began nailing planks down as we handed them up to him, and we finished with the roof planks just before lunchtime.

After we ate our lunch, we had our usual siesta and a swim, and this time we took off our pants before jumping into the water, so we didn't have to work all afternoon in wet jeans. And since it was so nice that day, we worked in just our under shorts the rest of the afternoon. It was cooler, and we sure weren't going to offend anyone out there in the middle of the river.

By evening we were just a few hours away from finishing the roof.

"One more day and it'll be done," Willie sang.

"Yep," Tone said, giving us one of his dazzling grins. "Tomorrow we'll finish and then we can move our stuff out here. Then we're 'gone fishing' the who-o-ole summer."

Willie brought his entire wardrobe with him the next morning: one shirt, two underwear shorts, and an extra pair of cut off bib overalls.

"You must have a lot of bib shorts," Tone said to Willie.

"Yeah, I keep growing taller but not fatter, so I just cut the legs off when they get too short. Yeah, I've got shorts for years," he said, grinning like a goof.

That day we hauled some of our gear with us, and we brought the metal pail that we intended to bury to keep our food cool. We put all of the stuff in the boat and took it across. After we finished nailing the tin on the roof and smeared tar on the nails, we dug a hole in the corner of the cabin so we could bury the metal pail. The sand was cool and damp a foot or so down.

With a good cover, it would serve to keep some of our food cool for a while at least. It surely would be cooler than having it sitting out.

We hung the door on its hinges, and slid the stovepipe up through the hole we cut in the roof over the stove, and tarred around it so it wouldn't leak.

We were about finished. We picked up all of the wood scraps and bent nails, and finally we were satisfied that the job was done! Our reward was lunch on the beach, and afterward we stripped off our clothes and went for a swim. Then we just lay in the sand and let the sun beat down on us.

"Ahh, this is the life," Tone sighed.

"Tomorrow we'll move in," I reminded him.

Day one – officially – of our summer adventure.

Chapter 20

Our biggest problem as a result of staying on the island was keeping our jobs with Mr. DeSilva. He didn't like the idea of us being gone all summer, but we had made the agreement with him that we would come back to town whenever he needed our help. Our fine boat made that arrangement quite workable because it paddled so easily and we could quickly make it back to town on rather short notice. But now that Willie would be on the island with us, we had a new problem to solve. He would have been Mr. DeSilva's messenger to send for us, so we had to find somebody else who could be trusted with the responsibility.

Willie suggested his friend, Ronnie. Ronnie lived just down the street and knew Mr. DeSilva because they were neighbors. He was eager to take the job when Willie told him that he'd probably get paid a nickel or a dime every time he was asked to carry a message to us.

So on the first morning of our adventure, Mr. DeSilva and Ronnie came with us to the river. We piled all of our food and blankets and other gear into Mr. DeSilva's big wagon, and the five of us headed out. Tone and I had bid our families farewell amid a few tears from our moms, but we assured them that we'd be back to town frequently because of our jobs, and to get more food.

Willie could hardly sit still as we drove along the high bank to the river. It would be good for him to live with someone besides girls for a while. His mom was a real nice lady who worked hard to keep the five kids fed and clothed. His dad had been a logger and was killed when Willie was just four years old, so he really needed some male companionship. He was such a fun kid to be with, and we were glad that we had invited him to share our adventure.

"If you guys ever need someone to help you on the island, let me know. I'm a good helper," Ronnie said as we neared the river.

"We'll keep that in mind, Ronnie. Maybe you can come and

stay with us sometime during the summer for a few days – if your mom says it's okay."

"No foolin'? Really? That would be great!"

We arrived at the riverbank and unloaded our gear. "Thanks, Mr. DeSilva," Tone said. "We appreciate the ride."

"You boys have fun, and keep an eye out for Willie. I'll send Ronnie down if I need you." He slapped the horses with the reins and started down the sand road. "Ronnie... you better come along now."

"I'm gonna stay and help them take the stuff across," Ronnie replied. "I can walk home. It's not that far."

We loaded the boat and all four of us climbed in. Willie and Ronnie sat in the middle on a pile of blankets and the rug. When we reached the island beach and had everything unloaded, Willie and Ronnie volunteered to carry it all to the cabin while Tone and I paddled back to the riverbank for the rest of the gear. By the time we got back, they had carried everything except the rug to the cabin.

"We piled it all outside," Willie said. "Figured you'd want to put the rug down first."

"Good thinking, Willie," I said.

We carried the rug up to the cabin and spread it out on the floor. It was just about perfect. One side was a little too long, so Tone cut it off with his Swiss Army knife. Then we cut a hole and fit it around the stove. We made sure the rug wasn't too close to the stove so it wouldn't catch on fire and burn down the cabin.

We stored the food in the buried pail and hung our hammocks in the back of the cabin away from the stove.

"We can build a little table here," Tone said. We started to cut planks for the table project, while Willie and Ronnie went off with the hatchet to gather some firewood for the evening.

Everything seemed to be in pretty good order, so we strolled down to the beach for a swim.

"Can you swim, Ronnie?" I asked.

"Like an fish," he said, grinning. He dropped his jeans in the sand, slipped off his underwear and dove into the river. He came up about ten feet away and laughed with glee. "This is so great! Aren't you guys coming in?"

It took Willie just seconds to step out of his bibs and he, too, was in the river splashing and laughing.

Tone and I just stood on the beach and watched the two kids playing for a while. "Ronnie sure is tan," I said to Tone. "Just like Willie"

"Suppose they've been swimming together a lot?" Tone nodded and grinned.

Tone and I shucked off our clothes and dove in. We were all having a great time. And when we came back on the beach, Tone volunteered, "I'll run up and make some sandwiches. You guys can wait here."

Willie lay back on the sand. "This is gonna be the best summer I've ever had."

"Well, Willie," I replied. "We're sure glad, too, that you can spend it with us."

Tone came back toting a plate stacked high with ham sandwiches. They disappeared rather quickly. It was getting late, and probably time for Ronnie to be heading for home.

"I'll row you across if you want," I offered.

"No need to," Ronnie said. "I'll just swim. It's not that far." He wrapped his clothes in a bundle and held them over his head with one hand and side stroked with the other. On the riverbank he dressed and waved goodbye. "You guys have fun," he called to us. "I'll see you as soon as somebody croaks."

We all laughed and waved to Ronnie.

"Well, guys, let's get everything straightened up in the cabin. Maybe we can do some fishing before suppertime."

Chapter 21

We spent part of the evening organizing, stashing, and tidying up in the cabin. We hung the two oil lamps from nails on the walls and rigged up three stools for when we ate inside at the table.

Outside on the beach, we decided that a fire pit would be nice for light and a little warmth on cool nights when we just wanted to sit and fish. Willie found our shovel and started digging.

There were lots of chores to keep us busy, but sorting our fishing gear was the next priority. We each had a fishing pole, a few hooks and sinkers, and a couple of spinners. We had a five hundred foot roll of braided twine and two hundred extra fishhooks, too. That, of course, was for making setlines to string across the channel in several places. Mr. Marcus at the General Store would take all the catfish we could catch in trade for essentials like flour and salt and things that we needed. He did a good business in fresh fish, but he never had enough to satisfy all of his customers. We were quite sure that we could do a good business, too, catching them.

We had a roll of chicken wire that was an important part of our fishing business plan. Our idea was to dig out a chunk of the bank of our island and build a wire fish pen right in the river. Then, as we caught fish, we'd put them into the pen until we had enough to make a trip to town worthwhile. We could clean them all at once, and it was the only way to keep a lot of fish from spoiling.

Puttering with all the little chores had kept us busy, and before we knew it, the sun was setting.

"Well, let's have some supper," I said, "and then we can try out our hammocks."

Our moms had provided us with several jars of canned beef, pork, chicken, peaches, pears, and several jars of jam. And Tone's mom had sent three big loaves of bread with us. We wouldn't starve – for a while, anyway. We finally decided on beef sandwiches.

After we ate, we walked down to the beach and sat in the sand. The frogs were chirping and the cicadas were singing and it was just about the prettiest evening that I had ever seen.

"Well, pals? Here we are," I said.

Tone smiled one of his big, dazzling smiles. "Our first night away from home."

"I bet my sisters are in my room snooping through all my good stuff," Willie sneered. But then he chuckled, realizing that his summer on the island was worth it.

We talked for a while and then decided that it must be bedtime. When we got back to the cabin we realized that we didn't have a place for Willie to sleep. With all of our careful planning, we had forgotten that one detail.

"Shit, I forgot all about that," I mumbled.

"Don't worry 'bout it," Willie said. "I can sleep on the floor."

"No, you're not going to sleep on the floor," Tone said. "You can sleep in the other end of my hammock. It's plenty long enough for both of us."

"Are you sure, Tone? I don't want to be in the way."

"Not a problem, Willie. There's plenty of room. If it doesn't work, we'll make you your own bed tomorrow."

Willie climbed up into the other end of Tone's hammock and snuggled down in his blanket. "Thanks, Tone, for letting me share your bed."

"No problem, Willie. I hope you're comfortable."

"Don't roll over in your sleep, or you'll crash to the floor," I laughed.

I turned down the lamp wick. The cabin plunged into darkness. I listened to Tone's breathing and soon it became slow and deep. I knew he had drifted off to sleep. Willie snored quietly, and I lay there thinking about how great it was to be here with these good friends.

I had just drifted off to sleep when a huge splash just outside in the river woke me again. It sounded like someone had dropped a big rock into the water.

"What the heck was that?" Tone said. The noise had awakened him, too.

"I'm not sure. It sounded like something fell into the river."

"You suppose someone is throwing stuff at us from the river bank?" Willie asked.

Just then, the same noise sounded again: Sploosh!

"Holy smokes! That was right outside!"

I felt around in the darkness until I found a match, struck it and lit the lamp. We all climbed out of our beds and inched our way to the door. Willie let Tone and me go first.

Cautiously, we stepped out into the night. I held the lamp toward the river.

Sploosh!

"I saw it," Willie said in a screaming whisper. "Over there!" He pointed toward the shore.

Something was moving through the water. It looked like a dog.

"It's a dog... swimming." Tone said.

Just as he said it, the dog slapped its tail on the water and dove for the bottom.

"No. It's a beaver," I said.

"Cripes! What's he doing?" Willie asked, shivering.

"I saw some chewed trees over on the other side of the island.

83

I'll bet he was going to come up here and chew some trees and found us in his territory. He's probably trying to scare us away."

"Have you ever seen the teeth on a beaver?" Willie quizzed. "Those scare me pretty good."

"Yeah," I laughed. "I wouldn't want to tangle with one of them."

"With that thing around," Willie said, "maybe I'll start wearing my shorts when I swim from now on."

Tone and I burst out laughing. "Willie, you can sure come up with some goofy ideas."

Willie's white teeth gleamed in the low light. He was really enjoying every minute of this.

"Let's go back to bed. I'm getting cold."

We hustled back inside and everyone got all nice and comfy again. I turned out the light.

"Good night, big brothers."

"Good night, Willie."

Chapter 22

I was still half asleep but I could tell it was morning. I didn't want to open my eyes and did my best to ignore the sunlight pouring in through the cabin window. I snuggled down in my warm blanket. A few minutes later, I heard a cracking sound. I opened my eyes to see Willie kneeling on the floor in the corner. He was wearing Tone's tee shirt and splitting some kindling with Tone's hatchet.

I glanced over at Tone. He, too, was awake, lying on his side watching Willie. Tone smiled. "Sounds like we've got a mouse in our house."

Willie peeked over his shoulder and saw us both watching him. He beamed a big smile. "Morning, guys. Thought I'd make a little fire to take the chill off."

"Good idea, Willie," I said. "Maybe put some water in the kettle to heat up, too." Willie grinned, put the kindling in the firebox and lit a match to it. A few minutes later, the kindling was crackling with flames, and he slid in a couple of small pieces of dry wood. He filled the kettle with water from a pail sitting in the corner, took off Tone's shirt and scrambled back into his blankets on the end of Tone's hammock.

"Dang! Willie," Tone yelled. "Your feet are cold. Keep them on your side of the bed."

Willie giggled and tried to put his cold feet even farther on Tone's end of the hammock. They playfully battled, kicking at each other for a while, and finally, Willie gave up. "I'm wide awake now. Might as well get up."

Since none of us had a clock, we had no idea of the time, but it didn't really matter. We had no place to be and nothing special to do, anyway. Our time was all ours.

Willie slipped on Tone's shirt again. It came to his knees and looked like a nightshirt.

"Think you're gonna wear my shirt all day?"

"Nope. Just till the cabin gets a little warmer. You should

know I never wear shirts or shoes in the summer time. It's bad enough to have to wear them in the winter."

"You're a real back to nature kind of kid, Willie."

Willie grinned and shrugged his shoulders. "I like not wearing a shirt and shoes. But even better, it drives my sisters crazy. They complain about it all the time, calling me a savage. I put my bare toes on one of them and they freak out." He laughed delightedly.

After I washed my face and brushed my teeth, I went outside to toss the water. I gazed about. "It's going to be a fantastic day," I announced to the others. "Not a cloud in the sky."

I lifted the lid off the buried cooler and pulled out six eggs and a slab of bacon. I sliced the bacon and soon it was sizzling in a frying pan. The cabin began to smell great. When the bacon was done, I took it out and cracked the eggs into the pan. Some of them broke, so I scrambled them all. "Soup's on!" I called out.

We all scooped up a plateful of eggs and bacon and sat at the table to eat. Willie couldn't stop grinning.

"What's so funny, Willie?"

"Nothing's funny. I'm just so happy being here with you guys instead of listening to my sisters whining and griping about everything I do."

Willie leaned over to the left, lifted his right leg and farted. He began laughing like he was crazy.

"Jeez, Willie. Now I see why your sisters gripe at you." We all laughed at Willie's rude manners.

"What are we gonna do today?" Willie asked.

"Well, I think we should make up our set lines so we can start catching some catfish. And maybe we should get some firewood cut ahead and stored in the corner, so if it rains we'll have enough dry wood. And probably a swim and a nap."

Life was good when you didn't have to worry about being somewhere and doing something at a certain time.

Chapter 23

After breakfast we washed the dishes and the frying pan and got everything put away. While Tone and Willie washed up, I took one end of each hammock loose from its hook on the wall and hung that end on the other hook. That made for a lot more room to move around. In the evening we'd just hook them up again.

It had warmed up, so we decided to continue our day with some of the outside chores. There was plenty of dead wood on the island to be cut up for firewood. If we gathered it all, it would be quite a while before we'd have to go to the riverbank for more.

When the firewood was all gathered and cut, Tone suggested that we make up some setlines. We took the spool of cord and our hooks down to the beach and sat in the sand. By then, the sun was up and it felt good on our bare backs. Willie was back in his favorite uniform – cut off bib overalls, no shirt and barefoot. Tone and I didn't bother to put any shoes on either, since the warm sand felt so good on our bare feet. We started wearing cut off jeans that day, too. Shorts were much more comfortable for summer wear.

"This is the life," Willie said, reassuring himself that he was enjoying his current situation.

"You seem mighty happy today, Willie," I said.

"You can't imagine. If I was home now, my sisters would be driving me crazy. Willie, do this. Willie, do that. Willie, quit burping. Willie, quit farting. Then they'd want to play house and I'm the daddy. Then they'd want to play dress up and put ribbons and stuff in my hair. I tell you, this is like getting out of prison on parole for me."

Tone and I had to laugh at the thought of Willie with ribbons in his hair. "Ribbons in your hair, Willie?" Tone teased. "They must look real cute with your cut off overalls."

After we got all the laughing out of our systems, we settled down to some serious work again.

"Watch, Willie," I said. "This is how you tie on the hooks for a setline." Willie watched closely as I doubled the cord, put the doubled line through the eye of a fish hook, tied a loose knot with the end of the cord around itself, slipped the hook through the loop that was left at the end, and pulled the knot tight. "There did you see how I did that? We'll put a hook about every two feet."

Willie measured two feet from my hook and expertly tied a copy of the knot onto another hook.

"You did that real good, Willie. Your hands are small and you're better at it than I am, already."

"I'll do them all if you want," Willie offered.

"No, Willie, you don't have to do them all," Tone said. "We'll help."

So we started making setlines about a hundred feet long with fifty hooks each and some extra line at each end to tie to a tree or roots to hold it in place. Some big lead sinkers would be attached when we put the lines in the river to keep them near the bottom where the catfish were. After a couple of hours we had three lines ready and rolled up each one on a cut off piece of plank.

"Now," I said, leaning back in a good stretch. "I think it's time for some lunch... and then maybe a swim and a siesta."

Back at the cabin, we considered our choices. "What shall it be?" I asked, as I peered down into the buried cooler. "Chicken? Or Pork?"

"Chicken," Willie blurted out quickly.

"Chicken's fine with me, too," Tone added.

The canned chicken was all cooked, and only needed to be warmed. We made sandwiches and didn't bother with plates. We just poured some water in the pan and left it for cleaning later, and headed for the beach.

The water was just perfect that day. We horsed around in the river for an hour, and then lay down in the sand on the beach. We were soon sound asleep.

I woke up some time later when I felt something cool dripping on the middle of my back. Willie was standing over me dripping river water from his cupped hands.

"Hey, you little rat," I yelled as I jumped up. Willie took off running, shrieking with laughter. That woke up Tone, and he joined in the chase up and down the beach. We'd just get close to Willie and he'd zig and zag and elude us. Off we'd go again. We kept up the pursuit until we finally captured him. He was laughing crazily as I took his hands and Tone took his feet. We carried him to the edge of the water, swung him back and forth a few times and then tossed him into the river. He loved it.

Laughing like a fool, winded from all the running, Willie staggered out of the water. "Well? What should we do now?" he asked, still ready for more.

"Let's get the fishing poles and try to catch some fish for supper."

"We don't have any bait," I reminded Tone.

"You get the poles rigged up," Tone said. "Willie and I can paddle to the riverbank and dig some worms."

At the cabin they found an empty jar to hold the worms. Tone put on his shorts and got into the back of the boat. Willie was about to jump in when Tone said, "Willie, you better put some clothes on. There's poison ivy on the riverbank, and if you get it on your weenie, it won't be funny." Willie grinned, ran to get his ever-present overalls, slid them on and jumped into the boat.

I watched them paddle across the river. There couldn't be two happier guys in the world right then. Actually, make that three.

Chapter 24

I had all three poles rigged up and ready to go, and had cut some forked sticks to prop up the poles in the sand when Tone and Willie paddled back across the channel.

"We got some nice, fat worms," Willie said as they pulled *Voyageur* up onto the beach. He raised the jar to show me the worms. We baited the hooks, threw the lines out into the current, and propped the poles with the forked sticks.

We dangled our feet in the water and watched the poles for the sign of a bite. Before long, the tip of the pole closest to Tone began moving just a little.

"Willie," Tone whispered. "See that?"

Willie nodded.

"Next time it does that, grab it and set the hook."

Willie scootched closer and put his hand a few inches from the pole. He was ready for action. Just a few moments later, the tip of the pole began bouncing again. Willie grabbed the pole and jerked the hook into the fish that was nibbling on the worm.

"I got him!" Willie shouted. He stood up and began reeling in the line. There was no doubting that he had hooked a pretty big fish, and as he reeled it in, he began stepping backwards away from the water. He was fifteen feet back and heading into the trees.

"Stay here, Willie! Where are you going?" I said, laughing at his odd maneuver.

Willie grinned and came back to the edge of the water to continue his battle with the fish. A few minutes later, a nice, tired catfish was splashing in the shallow water.

Tone waded in, grabbed the fish and tossed it up onto the sand. "Good job, Willie," he said, giving Willie a congratulating pat on the shoulder.

Willie's smile was about as wide as the river. "Well, I got *my* supper."

Tone and I laughed at that, and then baited the hook again and threw the line back into the current. It didn't take long to land three more catfish.

"That ought to be enough for supper," I said, "unless Willie eats a lot more than I think he can."

Willie patted his belly. "I'm not so big, but I can eat pretty good."

Willie went to the cabin to peel some potatoes while Tone and I cleaned the fish. We had just finished when Willie came out of the cabin and tossed the potato peels into the river. When he went back in, Tone glanced my way and smiled. "I'm glad we let Willie stay with us. He's a neat kid."

"Yeah, kinda like that little brother we never had, huh?"

Tone nodded and put his hand on my shoulder. "But I've got a pretty darn good *big* brother, two days older," he said.

When we came in, the stove was crackling and Willie was slicing potatoes into a pan with melting lard.

"Willie, where did you learn to be such a cook?"

"My mom taught all of us *girls* to cook," he said with a grin on his face. "When you're the only boy in five kids you have to learn to do your share, and I kinda like to cook. It's way better than washing dishes."

Willie added some sliced onions to the potatoes and tended to them so they didn't burn. Tone and I dipped the fish fillets in flour and dropped them into another hot pan. We soon had a delicious looking supper ready to devour.

"How about grace?" Willie said as we sat down to eat.

"You do the honors," Tone said.

Willie bowed his head and we all clasped our hands. "God, we thank you for this food and for the beautiful day we had. I thank you extra good for letting me stay here with Tone and Ladd, my two new brothers. Amen."

"Amen."

Willie looked up. Tears streaked his cheeks. "Thanks, guys. You're the best."

"We're glad you're here, Willie," I said.

Somehow, this seemed like the best catfish and fried

potatoes that I had ever tasted. When we had finished nearly all of it, Tone slid his stool back and rubbed his stomach. "I think I'm gonna explode."

I was stuffed, too. I couldn't eat another bite. But Willie was still shoveling it in. "There's still one piece of fish and a few potatoes left. Anyone want them?" He stared at us like we were wimps.

"Go ahead, Willie. They're yours."

He scooped the food onto his plate and it rapidly disappeared. He leaned back and let a gigantic belch that nearly shook the walls. We all laughed like crazy. When we finally quit laughing, Willie grinned and said, "Whoops, pardon me." We laughed again until we were almost sick.

If this first day was any indication of the fun we'd have the rest of the summer, there was no doubt that it would be great.

Chapter 25

After the supper dishes were washed and the cabin tidied up a bit, we sat on the beach and watched the sunset.

"Our first day is over," Tone sighed.

"And a good one it was," I said. I leaned back in the sand.

We just sat there without talking and watched the river flow by. Frogs began croaking and the splashing sounds of fish taking bugs off the surface of the river drifted across the calm, evening water. Dusk faded to darkness, and the air started to get a little chilly. "Let's go inside where it's warmer," I said as I slapped Willie on the back.

We lit the lamps and hung the hammocks back on their hooks. "You know what? We forgot to make a bed for Willie," I said.

"If Willie doesn't mind, he can sleep in the other half of my hammock again," Tone said. "I didn't even know he was there until he put his cold feet on me this morning."

"How about it, Willie? Is that okay with you?"

"It's great. I'm real comfortable there. Tone's feet are real warm, and they're pretty big too. They keep my little ones nice and warm," he said, grinning.

"Well, okay. Then we'll leave it at that," I replied. "I'm going to read for a while."

"What are you reading?" Tone asked.

"Mom gave me a copy of *Moby Dick* and *A Tale of Two Cities*."

"Why don't you read out loud, so we can hear it, too?" Willie said.

"Okay. Which one do you want to hear?"

"*Moby Dick*" Willie said with a little excitement in his voice. "I like fish stories."

With blankets all arranged, we got undressed and climbed into the hammocks in our underwear. I opened the book and began reading:

"Call me Ishmael. Some years ago - never mind how long precisely - having little or no money in my purse, and nothing in particular to interest me on the shore, I thought I would sail about a little and see the watery part of the world..."

Every time I looked up I'd see Willie watching me and listening intently. After about an hour, I noticed a noise from Tone's end of the hammock. His eyes were closed.

"Okay... that's enough for one night," I whispered to Willie and nodded toward Tone.

"Yeah, I'm getting pretty tired, too. G'night, Laddee."

"Good night, Willie. Have good dreams."

Hours later I woke to the rumble of thunder far off in the west. Half an hour after I had heard the first booms, lightning flashed, and it lit up the inside of the cabin. I lay there watching the lightning, and then I noticed that Willie was awake, too. His eyes were open wide, and he looked just a little frightened.

"Are you okay, Willie?"

"Yeah, I guess. But I'm not real happy when it storms," he said softly.

Then the wind roared and there was another loud thunder crash, and within seconds, a downpour of rain pounded on the tin roof. I got up, lit one of the lamps, and watched the roof to see if there were any leaks. Other than one small drip in the corner by the cooler, the roof seemed to be holding pretty well. I looked over at Willie. His head was under his blanket and I could see he was shivering.

"Willie, are you cold?"

"No. Just a little scared," his small voice came from under the blanket.

"Come on over here," Tone said.

"What?" Willie peeked from under the blanket.

"Come over here by me. We'll share this end until the storm is over."

Willie crawled to Tone's end of the hammock. Tone slid to the side and Willie lay down next to him. Tone put one arm around Willie as he snuggled down and pulled the blanket over them. "Now, just take it easy," Tone said, trying to comfort Willie. "I used to be scared of storms, too. In fact, I still am a little scared, so we'll just take care of each other. I feel safer when there's somebody close to me in a storm, too." When Willie seemed settled, Tone smiled and winked at me.

He was the bravest guy I'd ever known, and I knew he wasn't one bit afraid of storms. But he was such a good guy that he was willing to let Willie think he was afraid, so Willie didn't feel dumb for being scared. Willie put his free arm over Tone's chest and as he began to doze off he laid his head against Tone's shoulder. He was there to protect his big brother from the storm.

"I'm gonna turn out the light," I whispered to Tone. "Good night... again."

"Night." Tone returned.

"G'night," Willie murmured. As I snuffed out the light I could see a contented smile on his face. He wasn't afraid anymore.

Chapter 26

I was the first one awake the next morning. Tone was still sleeping with Willie snuggled up against him like a little puppy. I quietly rolled out of my hammock, got my shorts on, and went outside to see if the storm had done any damage. All I found was that the boat was half full of water. I went back inside the cabin and Tone and Willie were lying there talking. "Any damage outside?" Tone asked.

"Boat's half full of water," I said. "We'll have to remember to turn it over from now on."

Willie jumped out of bed, began chopping kindling and making a fire. I filled the kettle with water and got some eggs and bacon from the cooler for breakfast. Tone got up and hung the hammocks out of the way, and soon we were eating our breakfast and planning the day.

"I'll clean up the dishes," Tone said. "While I'm doing that, you guys can dig some more worms. Let's put out our setlines and see if we can catch some fish."

That sounded like a good idea.

After breakfast Willie and I went to empty the water out of *Voyageur*. As we tipped the boat over, Willie said, "That was pretty nice of Tone to let me sleep on his end during the storm."

"Tone likes you a lot," I told Willie. "He's a real good guy, and we've been best friends for all our lives. If you've got Tone for a friend, you're a lucky guy."

"I think I'm lucky to have *both* of you for friends." Willie smiled warmly and gave me an affectionate pat on the back.

While Willie gathered up the shovel and a can for the worms, I went to the cabin to chat with Tone. "That was pretty nice of you to share your bed with Willie," I said. "He really appreciated it."

Tone frowned just a little. "You know, Willie tries to act like he's a big kid, but he's only twelve, and he's still a little boy inside. If it made him feel safer, I was glad to do it." Tone's frown melted into a little smile.

Just then Willie came into the cabin carrying an empty lard pail that had previously held nails. "We can put the worms in this," he said, proud of his good find.

"Yeah! That'll work great, Willie. Let's shove off."

We paddled *Voyageur* to the shore and I dug while Willie picked up the worms. After the rain, they were up close to the surface, so it didn't take long to get the pail full.

On the way back to the island, Willie asked, "Have you ever used clams for bait?"

"Yeah, sometimes. Why?"

"A while back, me and some of my friends from school were wading in the shallow water upriver a little ways. We found a gravel bar and it was full of clams."

"How far upriver."

"Oh, maybe half a mile."

"Think you can find it again?"

"Sure. I know right where it is."

Tone had just finished the cleaning chores when we arrived back at the cabin.

"Willie says there's a clam bed upriver about half a mile from here," I explained to him. "Let's paddle up there and see if we can find it. We can use clams for bait on some of the hooks, and maybe we can find a good place to set a line up there, too."

"Good idea," Tone agreed.

With our three setlines, some extra sinkers and the bucket of worms, we pointed *Voyageur* up the river in search of Willie's clam bed. Like a dream, the boat slid through the water with very little effort, even though we were paddling against the current. When we had gone some distance, Willie pointed and shouted, "There! Right over there! By that sandy beach. That's where the clams were!"

We beached the boat right next to the gravel bar that was in shallow water, and close to the shoreline. We waded in and began feeling for clams with our toes.

"Ronnie and me and the other guys were just fooling around here, and we found a bunch of clams," Willie said as he reached down and pulled a clam out of the water. Before long I found one with my toes, and so did Tone. In another ten minutes we had plenty of them to bait our lines. Willie sat in the bottom of the boat, pried them open with my Swiss Army knife, took the meat out and cut it into little chunks to put on the hooks.

Meanwhile, Tone and I paddled along and checked the water depth with our paddles every so often until we found a good channel. "Let's put the first one here," I suggested.

At the shore, we tied the end of the line to big tree root that stuck out over the water, and marked the spot with a marrow strip of cloth we cut from an old tee shirt so we could find the line the next day. I handled the boat, keeping it from drifting downstream, and moving us slowly away from the bank, while Willie and Tone baited the hooks – one with a clam, and the next with a worm – and paid the line out over the end of the boat. With two of them baiting the hooks, it didn't take long to get the whole line baited and stretched out. There wasn't anything to tie the end to out in the middle of the river, so we put a big bunch of sinkers on the end of the line and dropped it into the water.

"There. One down, two to go."

We found two more good spots to set out the other lines on the way back toward our island. We were back *home* just in time for lunch, our usual swim and a siesta on the beach. The rest of the afternoon we just sat in the sand and fished and talked and laughed. Willie whittled on a chunk of wood trying to make a white whale.

That night we had some homemade soup that mom sent with us, and later we decided to play cards. We had a deck of cards and a cribbage board with pegs for three players. Willie didn't know how to play, so we gave him a few quick lessons. He seemed to get the hang of it, so we played three-handed cribbage and had a lot of fun.

After a few hands, Willie counted his points. "Let's see, fifteen two, fifteen four, and a pair is eight." He moved his marker eight holes.

"Wait a minute," Tone protested. "Fifteen two, fifteen four, and a pair is *six*, not eight."

"Oh! Sorry," Willie apologized, and moved the counter back one hole.

"*Two* holes back, not one."

Willie moved his peg back.

On the next hand, Willie counted his points and moved *Tone's* counter backward.

"Hey! That's not your counter. That's mine. And you moved it the wrong way."

Willie tried to look serious and confused, but he couldn't keep a straight face and started to snicker.

"You little cheater! You're not so dumb. You're cheating."

Willie just about fell off his stool laughing. "I've been playing cribbage since I was six years old," he said, laughing so hard he could barely talk. Tone and I learned our lesson quickly, too – not to trust Willie's innocence from then on when it came to cards.

Another half hour and we started to yawn. Willie said, "If you guys are ready, I think it's time for bed. But Ladd? Can you read a little? I'd like to hear more about that big whale."

"Sure, Willie. I'll read till we can't stay awake."

We got undressed and Tone climbed into his hammock. Willie climbed in and snuggled down beside him. Tone looked at me and grinned. I guess Willie liked it better on that end.

We were soon following the adventures of Ishmael and Captain Ahab aboard the *Pequod*. And soon I noticed that Tone was asleep.

"Comfortable, Willie?" I whispered.

Willie nodded and smiled.

I set the book aside, shut off the lamp and pulled the covers up around my shoulders.

"Night, Willie," I whispered.

"G'night, Laddee."

Chapter 27

The next morning I was the first one up again. Willie and Tone were still sleeping, Willie with his arm across Tone's chest and looking pretty comfortable. I tried to be quiet as I started a fire, but Tone woke up.

"Looks like you've got a new best friend," I said.

Tone nodded and yawned. "I think this is maybe a little new for him. Probably the first time he's ever slept away from home, and it does get pretty dark out here. It's not a problem, though. He's so small I hardly know he's here."

Willie rustled in his sleep and a few moments later he opened his eyes. It took him a second to figure out where he was, and then he saw Tone smiling at him. "Hey, good morning, Tone. Jeez. I don't think I ever slept so good. You kept me nice and warm."

Tone chuckled. "Well, I'm glad you were comfortable."

After breakfast we paddled upriver to see if we had caught any fish on the setlines. A couple of large buckets in the boat would keep them alive if we had. We arrived at the first line tied to the root and Tone lifted the cord out of the water as I backed the boat away from the bank. Willie re-baited each hook if it was empty. After six or seven empty hooks, a nice, fat catfish came up on the next one. Tone took it off, passed the hook to Willie for bait, and put the catfish in a bucket he filled with river water. As we worked our way to the end, we found four more catfish, a couple of carp, and a sucker. We threw the sucker and the carp back in the river.

"That wasn't too bad," Tone said. "Let's try the next one."

On the next line we had six catfish and on the last one we had another six. "Wow," Tone exclaimed. "Sixteen catfish in one day. Not bad at all."

I turned the boat downriver toward the island, "If we get three or four more lines out, we could get twenty or more a day," I speculated.

Our good luck with our first try at setlines was quite encouraging. We hustled back to the island, put the catfish in the chicken wire pen to keep them alive, had some lunch and then sat in the sand and assembled three more setlines. Willie had really caught on to tying the hooks, and he could do it twice as fast as Tone and me put together. "You guys got such big fingers," he teased. "You need little ones like mine for this kind of work."

Tone ruffled his hair. "Why do you think we brought you along?"

Willie grinned and punched Tone's leg.

When the setlines were finished, we decided to fish from our beach for a while. We felt like having fish for supper again and didn't want to eat any of our grocery fish if we didn't have to. In the next couple of hours we caught four nice cats and a good-sized walleye. It was getting close to suppertime, so Willie went to light a fire in the stove and began making his delicious fried potatoes. Tone and I cleaned the fish. When we got to the cabin, the aroma from the potatoes cooking made our bellies grumble.

"How about a can of beans with supper, too?" I asked.

"Yeah, I love beans," Willie said. "They're my favorite vegetable."

As usual, we had cooked enough food to feed a small village, but rather than wasting any of it, we ate till we were ready to bust. Willie polished off the last piece of fish and most of the beans. He leaned back and patted his belly. "Whew! Stick a fork in me. I'm done," he declared.

Tone and I burst out laughing. "Willie, there's never a dull moment with you around."

We let our supper settle beside a nice fire down on the beach. Even though it was getting dark, the fire gave off enough light for me to read more of *Moby Dick* to Tone and Willie. But eventually, the air chilled to the point of being uncomfortable.

"It's getting cold, and I'm ready for bed," Tone said.

"Me too," Willie chimed in.

We doused the fire, went back to the cabin and hung the

hammocks. When everyone was settled in, I shut off the lamp and the cabin was quiet.

"Good night, guys," I said.

"Good night," said Tone.

Willie farted one of the biggest farts I'd ever heard.

Tone began laughing so hard that he fell out of his hammock. "Willie you nasty little thing. What a pig!"

I lit the lantern. Willie was laughing so hard his face was wet with tears. "Who me?" And he let go with another.

We spent the next half hour laughing and every time we'd settle down, Willie would let another one blast.

"That's the last time you get any beans, Willie!"

"Awe, come on. I never get to do that at home. All my sisters have a fit."

"I can see why they pick on you now, Willie."

"I'll be good. I promise."

"You better be good or you'll be sleeping with Ladd." Tone was trying to be serious.

It was quiet for a while, and I was just dozing off when Willie let another blast. I could hear him chuckling in the dark for the next half hour.

Chapter 28

When we checked our lines the next morning, we had thirteen more catfish.

"That makes twenty nine," Tone said. "I think we should clean them and take them to town today."

"Good idea. We're out of eggs and other stuff, too. And we'll see what kind of a deal Mr. Marcus will give us before we get too many fish. If he tries to gyp us, we'll have to find another market for them."

We went back to our island, built a makeshift fish-cleaning table with a couple of planks and went to work. When we were finished, we had one pail full of catfish meat, and one pail full of heads and guts. "We'll dump the guts in the river on the way," I said. "If we dump it right here, we'll have turtles all over the place."

We packed a clean towel on top of the fish and loaded them and the guts in the boat. We gathered up all of the empty canning jars into a sack so we could drop them off at home, and if we were lucky, we'd get more full ones to bring back to the island.

Even with a heavy load going upstream, *Voyageur* slid through the water with not much effort. When we got near town we pulled the boat up on the shore. Tone and I took hold of the two handles on the bucket of fish and Willie carried the sack with the empty jars. It was a hot June day and we were all shirtless and barefoot as we walked down the main street of town to Mr. Marcus' market.

"Well, just look at you guys. You look like some lost sailors," Mr. Marcus said as we entered the store. "You guys must be having a lot of time in the sun. You sure are getting brown."

We looked at each other, and then at our reflections in a mirror hanging behind the counter. It was the first time we'd seen ourselves for over a week. We were surprised at how tan we had become. Seeing each other every day, we hadn't noticed how dark we were getting. My hair was sun bleached nearly blonde, and then I realized that Willie's normally blonde hair was almost white. Of course, Tone was naturally darker because of his Italian heritage.

"Wow, I guess this all happened gradually, and we didn't even notice," I said. "Looks like we've been stranded on an island."

"We *have* been on an island," Tone laughed. "Did you forget?"

"Well, what have you brought me?" Mr. Marcus asked.

"We've got twenty nine nice catfish," I said.

"*Real* nice ones. And they're fresh too," Willie said like a true salesman. "Just cleaned this morning before we came here."

Mr. Marcus grinned at Willie. He gave a little whistle when he removed the towel from the pail. "Those *are* real nice, boys. Just cleaned you say?"

"They were still swimming about two hours ago," Willie replied.

Mr. Marcus weighed a stainless steel pan on his scale. Then he put the catfish in the pan and weighed it again.

"Those are real nice fish, and you did a good job cleaning them." He did some figuring in his head and said, "You've got thirty-three pounds. I charge twenty cents a pound, so I'll give you twelve. I'll make a nice profit, and you boys will have some pretty good wages, too."

"That's three dollars and ninety-six cents," Willie said.

Quite amazed, I stared at Willie. "You're pretty sharp with numbers, aren't you?"

"Yeah, I can figure in my head pretty good." And then he turned his focus on the storekeeper again. "Mr. Marcus, we plan on spending our money here, so since we're kind of employees, don't we get a discount on our purchases?" He winked at me.

"You're a pretty shrewd little fellow, aren't you?" Mr. Marcus rubbed his chin and pleasantly smiled. "Okay. I'll take five percent off everything you buy."

Willie grinned.

We started gathering our groceries – a bag of flour, salt, a can of lard, a slab of bacon, a chunk of hard salami, some sausages, three dozen eggs, a big chunk of cheese, and some tea. Willie put three cans of beans on the counter.

"Oh no! No more beans for you," Tone scolded with a silly grin.

"Aw come on, guys. I like beans," Willie whined with a similar silly grin. "Remember the discount that I got for us? That more than pays for the beans."

Tone ruffled Willie's hair. "Okay, squirt. You can get your beans."

Our bill came to just over three dollars, so we still had some credit coming. "Can you just put that on the books for us, Mr. Marcus?" I asked.

"No problem, boys. It's nice doing business with you, and bring more fish any time. We can all make some money on this little enterprise."

We packed our groceries in the empty pail and Willie carried the extra that didn't fit. Tone patted Willie on the back as we marched down the street. "You're quite the clever little businessman."

"Hey, you gotta know how to barter when you grow up with four sisters," Willie said, grinning. "Marcus will make plenty off those fish, anyway. And that little discount won't hurt him a bit."

"Whatever would we do without you, Willie?" Tone said as he put his arm across Willie's shoulders.

We headed down the street toward our homes. We had to let our families know we were still alive.

Chapter 29

Our first stop was at Willie's house. His mom, quite surprised to see us, hugged and kissed Willie much to his embarrassment. A minute later, she invited us in. "Come have something to eat. You boys *must* be hungry."

Looking more like some theatrical troupe portraying South Seas island natives, we sat at the kitchen table as she made us some sandwiches. Then she came with a big slice of fresh apple pie for each of us.

"I can't get over how tan you boys are," she exclaimed. "Are you having fun out there?"

"Ma, it's great! Tone and Ladd are the best guys in the whole world." Willie could barely contain his enthusiasm.

His mom directed her attention to Tone and me. "Is he behaving himself? He can be a bit of a pill, sometimes."

"Maaaaaaaaaaa!"

"He's a good kid, and he's a lot of help," I returned. "And he's a pretty darn good cook, too."

Willie's blushing didn't show much through the tan, but it was there.

"I hope he's minding his manners," his mom continued. "He thinks it's real funny to pass gas in front of his sisters. He's not doing that to you, is he?"

A sudden look of terror came over Willie, thinking that we *might* tell his mom the truth.

"No," Tone lied. "He's been a perfect gentleman."

Willie let out his held breath, winked, at and gave Tone a thumbs up behind his mom's back.

We finished our lunch and announced that we had to be moving on. Willie's mom gave us the rest of the apple pie, some fresh bread and several jars of canned beef and pork to add to our grocery load.

"We'll stop back next time we bring fish," Willie said.

His mom hugged him and kissed him on the cheek. "Be a

good boy, Willie," she said.

"Love ya, Ma."

We stopped at Tone's house next. His mom had just taken fresh cookies from the oven; naturally, we had to sample a few.

"You guys look like natives...all tan and almost naked," she said. "The island life must agree with you. You all certainly look healthy."

"We're outside in the sun most of the day, and we just wear shorts most of the time," I said. "So I guess we're bound to get pretty tan."

"How's the cabin working out?"

"It's great, Mom. Just what we need – not too big and not too small – just perfect... and it keeps the rain out."

Before we went to my house, Angela insisted that we take a bag of cookies and two more loaves of fresh bread. We had received compliments on how healthy we appeared, so we didn't think we looked undernourished, but of course, we accepted the food, anyway.

"Thanks, Mom. We'll see you next trip to town."

My mom had baked a cake that morning. She saw us coming across the yard, and had three big pieces waiting for us on the kitchen table.

"My goodness, Ladd! I've never seen you so tan. You must spend a lot of time in the sun." Mom had hugs and kisses for all of us.

"Yeah, Ma, we do. We're outside all day long fishing and swimming."

"Are you taking good care of Willie?" she asked Tone.

"Yeah, Ma Two. We take real good care of him. We have to change his diaper a couple of times a day, but that's not so bad."

Willie cuffed Tone aside the head and we all had a good laugh.

Mom put her arms around Willie and gave him another big hug. "If these boys pick on you, just come back here and you can stay with me."

Willie grinned. "Yes, Ma." He stuck his tongue out at Tone.

We left my house with two more jars of canned chicken, three jars of strawberry jam, and a cake. By the time we made it back to the boat we were nearly exhausted from carrying all the food we had acquired. And we were all full as ticks, too, from all the treats we ate during the visit. That didn't help, either.

We piled all of the food into *Voyageur* and paddled down the river. "Let's get home," Willie said. "We're already late for our siesta."

"Aye aye, captain. Home it is."

As we made our way back to the island, I glanced over my shoulder to see Willie sitting in the bottom of the boat, eyes closed and head drooping forward. He was a tired little voyageur.

The journey to town and back had tired us out more than we realized. After we stashed all of our booty, our daily swim was much shorter than usual, and our nap on the beach, a little longer.

That evening, we didn't feel like cooking, so we built a fire in our fire pit on the beach and roasted sausages. They made delicious sandwiches. We ate the rest of the apple pie from Willie's mom and settled down for the evening.

"Can you read to us Ladd?" Willie asked. I picked up *Moby Dick* and began reading the scene where Ishmael was to share a hotel room and a bed with Queequeg, and saw him for the first time:

"Who-ee debil you?" Queequeg at last said. "You no speak-ee, damm-ee I kill-ee." And so saying, the lighted tomahawk began flourishing about me in the dark."

Willie's eyes were big as saucers as I described the tattooed Queequeg. When I had been reading for a couple of hours, we all began yawning and we decided it was time for bed.

As I turned off the lamp I heard Willie say to Tone in a voice as deep as he could make, "Who debbil you? You no speak-ee, I fart-ee!"

We laughed ourselves to sleep.

Chapter 30

During the night, rain started to fall. It wasn't a big storm with lots of thunder and lightning, but a hard, steady rain that just kept pounding on the roof hour after hour.

The morning was gray and foggy. Rain was still coming down. It was like stepping right into the middle of a cloud.

"Looks like we're inside for the day," I said as I peered through the window in the door.

Since we had so much new food, we really had a feast for breakfast – eggs, bacon and tea, and then we ate a big piece of my mom's cake for desert.

The air was just chilly enough inside the cabin that we built a small fire in the stove. We wore our shirts for the first time in many days, and Willie was wearing one of Tone's that came to his knees. We played three-handed cribbage, and after a couple of hours when we were tired of playing cards, we re-hung the hammocks and took a nap.

I resumed reading *Moby Dick* that afternoon. We were near the end where Captain Ahab is trying to kill the whale:

"Sink all coffins and all hearses in one common pool! And since neither can be mine, let me then tow to pieces, while chasing thee, though tied to thee thou dammed whale! Thus, I give up the spear." Ahab was thrown out of the boat, ere the crew knew he was gone."

I looked up from the book and Willie was staring at me with his mouth agape. "And that's the end? He went overboard hooked to the whale?"

"Yes, Willie. Ahab went mad and nothing else mattered to him except to kill the whale."

"Wow! Good story."

Later that afternoon I started reading *A Tale of Two Cities*. The rain fell steadily all day. Just before dark, Tone said, "Let's go down and make sure the boat's okay."

"Good idea. If this rain keeps up, the river will rise, and we sure as heck don't want it to float away."

At the beach we decided to carry *Voyageur* up to the trees by the cabin. It would be about three feet higher above the water there, and much safer.

"I'm gonna tie this rope on it just to be sure," Willie said. He tied one end of the rope to the boat seat and the other around a tree.

"Do you think the water will get this high, Willie?"

"I'd rather not find out by losing the boat."

We thought about that for a few minutes. Willie had the right idea. We put the boat up into the crotch of two trees and tied it there to further ensure its safety.

It was warm and comfortable back inside the cabin. We all changed into dry clothes, and by then it was time for supper. The hot beef and boiled potatoes tasted great on such a miserable night.

When we went to bed it was still pouring rain, and the next morning it still hadn't let up. Through the window in the door we could see our beach was completely under water.

"Good thing we moved the boat," Tone said.

The rain never stopped as we passed the day slowly, eating, sleeping and playing cards. By evening the river had risen up to the edge of the trees. We stepped to the edge of the water. Tone stuck a stick in the sand. "We'll see how fast it's rising," he said.

Two hours later, the water was up another half a foot.

"Boys," I said. "If it keeps coming up like this, we might have water in the cabin."

We were worried about getting flooded out, but there was really nothing we could do about it. We checked on the boat and it was still high and dry. The water would have to raise four or five feet more to get to *Voyageur.*

"If the water gets that high," Willie said, "we're out of here!"

We all had a hard time getting to sleep that night. The rain still hadn't let up, and naturally, we were worried about what would happen if the water kept rising. The boat was our salvation if the cabin was flooded, but we knew even that was risky business in raging floodwater.

Sometime during the night I woke to a scary, moaning sound from outside the cabin. I sat up in my hammock and listened. Willie saw me sit up. "Ladd, did you hear that?"

"Yeah. What the heck was it?"

"Sounded like someone or something that's hurt," Tone said. Just then the sound came again, and this time it was more of a whimpering.

By then we were all out of our hammocks trying to look through the windows. I lit the lamp, but the glare of the lamp reflected back from the glass. I couldn't see anything.

Just then the sound came again. It seemed to be just outside the door. "It's right out there," I said.

Though the rain was still pouring down, I opened the door and held the lamp up. A little light might help us to identify what was making the noise. Willie sprinted over by me and peered out into the darkness. "Look there," he shouted, pointing to the left. "See those eyes shining?"

Tone joined us and we all looked where Willie was pointing. There in the low, overhanging branches of a tree was a little dog, clinging to a bunch of driftwood that had snagged there. "It's a puppy! He's in that tree," Willie squealed.

The little dog had somehow managed to climb up onto the driftwood caught in the branches, but he was barely hanging on. He looked terrified. As we watched the floodwater pushing against the bobbing driftwood, he lifted his head and let out a mournful cry. He knew we were there, and he was asking us for help.

"We gotta help him," I said.

"That current is pretty bad," Tone said, surveying the swirling water. We can't wade out there. If we get caught in that current we'll be swept off the island."

"Tie that rope around my waist," Willie blurted. "I'll go grab him and you guys can pull me back."

"That current is mighty strong, Willie."

"Well, we can't just let him drown! Tie me up! Hurry!"

Even though we knew it was risky – downright dangerous – Willie was determined to save that puppy, and if we didn't tie the rope around him like he demanded us to do, we were afraid he'd attempt the rescue on his own. So we tied the rope around his chest and he stepped off into the water that was now within only a few feet from the cabin door. "Brrr! It's cold," he yelled. As he waded farther into deeper water, we could see he was struggling with the current, and we considered pulling him back right then.

"Come on fella. I'm gonna help you," we heard him say to the dog, and it sounded as if the dog was answering him with a joyous whine. We couldn't stop him now. He was so close, and so determined. We just gave him more rope.

Willie was up to his armpits in the swirling water when he finally got close enough to grab the dog. He was just about to pick the dog off his floating life raft when the frightened pooch panicked and tried to jump into his arms. The instant he hit the water, the puppy disappeared out of range of our light. Willie dove into the black water after him. Tone and I held onto the rope tightly, probably more frightened at that moment than Willie was. We couldn't see him, but we could feel Willie tugging on the rope, wanting more slack, so we let a little more slip through our hands. Seconds seemed like hours. Then, we could just barely see Willie on the other side of the tree with the dog in his arms. The puppy's front legs wrapped around Willie's neck and he was holding on for dear life. "Pull me back!" Willie shouted.

Willie struggled against the current as we began pulling. He couldn't get his footing because the water was too deep and swift, so he just lay over on his back and we reeled him in like a big fish. He had the puppy wrapped in his arms, holding it tightly against his chest, keeping him out of the water as best he could. We were making some progress when they both went under water. He came up a few seconds later still clutching the dog and sputtering. "Pull harder," he yelled. "Hurry up! I'm freezing my balls off out here."

We kept pulling him in until he reached shallower water where he could touch bottom. "Stop pulling," he called out. "I can feel bottom now," he said as he struggled to his feet and waded to us. Tone took the puppy from him and I untied the rope.

"Come on," I said to Willie. "Let's get in out of the rain."

Willie was shivering so violently that I had to help him walk inside. I threw a couple of logs into the embers in the stove and grabbed a couple of dry towels. Tone used one to dry off the dog, and I wrapped the other one around Willie. He was still shivering uncontrollably. He stripped off his wet clothes, and with the big towel I dried him off and rubbed his back and arms to get some blood flowing again. Once he stopped shivering, he put on some dry underwear and one of Tone's shirts. I guided him closer to the stove, and snugged his blanket around his shoulders.

"Is the dog okay?" Willie asked through chattering teeth.

"He's cold and shivering, but he seems to be okay," Tone said. He had the dog all wrapped in a dry towel with just his nose and face sticking out.

He brought the pup to Willie so he could hold him and get warm by the fire.

"How's that little fella?" Willie gently hugged the critter. "You're safe now. We'll take good care of you."

The dog licked Willie's face, gave a contented little groan, and snuggled down into his arms.

"I think you've got a new friend," I said.

Willie smiled pathetically. "Poor little guy. He sure was lucky to get caught in those branches. I wonder where he came from."

"We'll probably never know," Tone said. "But it looks like he's got a home now."

"Can we keep him?" Willie asked.

"You saved him, Willie. It's up to you."

Willie beamed. "Wow. I've always wanted a dog. Of course, I want to keep him."

"What are you gonna call him?"

Willie thought for a minute. "Ahab. How about that? Like in *Moby Dick.*"

"And he's probably hungry," Tone suggested. "Better find him something to eat."

We found some bread and a piece of salami from the cooler. Tired as he was, he gulped the food down.

"See," Tone said. "He was famished. Probably hasn't eaten for a long time."

Willie climbed into the lower end of Tone's hammock with the puppy snuggled on his chest. Ahab closed his eyes and gave a big sigh.

"I think he's pretty glad to be here," Willie said. He wrapped his arms around little Ahab and covered him with his blanket. He was smiling like a proud papa as I turned off the light.

Chapter 31

Ahab was still sleeping soundly on Willie's chest when I woke up the next morning. It looked as though neither of them had moved a muscle all night. They'd both had a pretty rough time, so I guess they deserved a good night's sleep. But as soon as I stirred a bit, the dog was awake, too. He stared at me for a few seconds, and then started licking at Willie's face. Willie jumped at first, and his face twisted into an awful grimace as his hand tried to brush away the intruder. But then his eyes popped open and reality struck. He broke out into a big smile. "Good morning Ahab, how are you today?" The little dog's tail was wagging so fast I thought it was going to dislocate, or maybe fly off.

"It would be my guess," I said to Willie, "that Ahab needs to go outside."

"You gotta go pee?" Willie said to the dog. Ahab was jumping up and down, not sure what Willie was talking about but glad to be talked to. "Okay. Let's go." Willie got out of bed and opened the door to let Ahab out, but the dog slunk back away from the door. "No, you don't have to leave," Willie said. "Just go pee. Come on. I'll go with you." He coaxed the dog out with him and they both did their morning duty.

"How's the water?" Tone asked, still in his hammock when Willie came back in.

"Well, it's stopped rising, and it's not raining anymore," Willie said. "Looks like the sun is going to shine. Maybe the flood is over."

"Just in time too," I said. "Another foot and we'd have had a flooded cabin."

We built a fire in the stove and made breakfast. Ahab was ravenously hungry and ate his share like he had been starved for a month. "I wonder when he last had something to eat," I said.

Tone picked up Ahab and held him on his lap. "So what are you?" he said as he appraised the dog. Ahab was surely a mixed breed, and a big part of him was some kind of terrier. He was small and had perky ears and an inquisitive face. His hair was a little longer than most terriers so maybe he had a cocker spaniel as a close relative. He was mostly brown with a few patches of black and a white patch right in the middle of his forehead. "I think he's surely not a purebred... but he's kind of cute," Tone said.

"He's cute as the Dickens and his parents don't mean a thing," Willie said defensively. And to the dog he said, "Don't let Tone make you feel bad. You're a handsome boy and I'm glad you came to live with us." The dog's tail wagged furiously.

"You can sure tell that he likes you, Willie. Of course, you saved him and he'll never forget that." Willie hugged his dog.

"Toneeeeeee, Laddeeeee," we heard someone shouting from the riverbank. "Mr. DeSilva needs you." We poked our heads out the cabin door and there was Willie's buddy, Ronnie, on the bank across the channel.

"Hi, Ronnie. See my new dog?" Willie shouted as he picked up Ahab and showed him to Ronnie.

"Real nice, Willie. Can you guys come and dig a grave today?" he said to Tone and me.

"Sure. We'll come right away," I said.

Willie looked at us and said, "Can I stay here? I don't want to leave Ahab alone right away."

"Sure. Maybe Ronnie wants to spend the day with you. Why don't you ask him?"

Willie shouted over to Ronnie, "Do you want to come over and spend the day with me and Ahab? Tone and Ladd will go dig the grave, and you can go home when they get back."

"Can you guys tell my mom where I am?" Ronnie shouted.

"Sure. We'll stop and tell her," I said. "Just wait there and we'll come and get you in the boat."

We paddled over, picked up Ronnie, and dropped him off at the island. "We'll be back before dark. You guys have fun. Better stay out of the water for now – the current is pretty fast."

"See you later," they said.

"And don't eat all of our food, either," Tone called out as we paddled away.

We headed *Voyageur* upriver. The current was stronger than usual but we still made it back to town faster than if we had walked. With the boat pulled way up onto the shore we hustled toward Mr. DeSilva's funeral home, stopping at Ronnie's house first to let his mom know he was at the island with Willie. She thanked us, and we went on our way.

"Ah! The natives have returned," Mr. DeSilva said as we walked into the mortuary. We were barefoot and shirtless as usual.

"Oh, we're sorry, Mr. DeSilva. We should have worn our shirts and shoes."

"Not to worry, boys. The dearly departed here don't care, and I surely don't, either. Since you're here, why don't you help me slide Mr. Packard into his box, and then you can get started with the grave. The funeral is at one o'clock this afternoon, so if you can just hang around until they're done, you can fill the grave and you won't have to make another trip back to finish."

"That'll work out just great, Mr. DeSilva. Are the shovels and stuff in the wagon?"

"All is ready. Just go ahead. I've marked the grave site as usual."

After we got Mr. Packard into the casket, we drove the wagon to the cemetery and found the stake with the cloth tied to it. Not much more than two hours later, the grave was ready. We drove the horses and wagon to the back of the cemetery and rested in the shade until the hearse and mourners showed up for the burial. After everyone had left, we lowered the casket into the grave and filled it in. We were back at Mr. DeSilva's by just after three o'clock.

"Good work boys." Mr. DeSilva handed us two dollars. "How's life on the river?"

"Two dollars! Wow, Mr. DeSilva. That's more than we agreed on."

"You boys are good help. I've decided to give you a raise," he said. "So the river life is okay?"

"It's great, Mr. DeSilva. We're having a great time."

"How's Willie doing?"

"He's a good kid. We really like him," I said. "He's got a dog now, too. He's real happy being out there with us."

"That's nice of you boys to take him in. He's had a tough time, you know. His daddy was killed when he was so young, and he's had to grow up in a house full of women. He needs some big brothers like you."

"He's fun to be with, and he sure isn't afraid to do his share of the work, either, so we're glad to have him there," Tone said.

"Harvey Honer sure took a shine to him," Mr. DeSilva said. "I think he reminds Harvey of his own boy who died."

"He's a real nice man," I said. "Willie likes him a lot, too."

Tone poked me in the ribs. "We should really be getting back to the island so Ronnie doesn't have to walk home in the dark."

As usual, I had to agree with Tone's good judgment. "Thanks, Mr. DeSilva. And let us know when you need us again."

"I will, boys. Have a good time."

The water level had dropped a lot during the day and when we pulled up to the island, Ronnie and Willie were in the river by the beach playing catch with a stick while Ahab tried to get it from them.

"Hi, guys," Willie greeted us. "Come on in. The water's nice today."

We shucked off our clothes and joined them. We horsed around for a while and then Tone went under water and Ronnie climbed up on his shoulders. I went under and Willie got on my shoulders, and then we had a 'Giant War.' Tone and I would wade toward each other with the two little guys on our shoulders, and they would try to make the other fall off into the water. We played until we were exhausted.

It was getting late. I thanked Ronnie for coming to us with Mr. DeSilva's message and tossed him a quarter for his effort.

"But Mr. DeSilva already gave me a dime," he said.

"That's okay. You're a good messenger. It's worth it to us."

Tone paddled him across the channel in *Voyageur*.

"I'll see you guys again... as soon as somebody dies," he said, and off he went.

When all was quiet again, I said to my island companions, "Well, I think it's time for some supper, and then a little reading, and then a good sleep. It's been a pretty full day."

Chapter 32

"**B**etter go take a look at our setlines," Tone suggested the next morning. "We haven't checked them since the flood. They might have been washed away."

We paddled upstream to the gravel bar, collected a bucketful of clams, dug up some worms on the riverbank, and located the line marked with the strip of white cloth tied to the roots. But when Tone pulled it up, it was only about three feet long – the rest of the line with the hooks was gone. He held up the end of the line; it looked like it had been cut. "Something must have gotten tangled in it during the flood," Tone speculated.

"Might as well put out a new one... as long as we're here," I suggested.

Willie baited the hooks as Tone tied the new line to the roots and started feeding it into the water. When he dropped the anchor of lead sinkers at the end, he said, "Okay... let's check the rest of them."

We went to the next line and it, too, was gone. Only a short end remained.

"I'll bet they're all gone," Willie said.

We tied on a new line at the same place, baited it and moved down river to the last location. The line was still there, but the hooks were tangled with grass, leaves, and a lot of garbage. We cleared out all the trash and re-baited the hooks.

We still had one of our new lines left to set out. Tone thought we should find another spot somewhere below our island. Willie and I agreed.

About a quarter of a mile down river past the cabin, we found a nice channel between two islands. We tied one end of the line at the edge of one island, strung the baited hooks across and tied the other end to a small tree on the other island.

"Well," Willie grinned. "Back home for some lunch... and maybe a siesta?"

"For such a skinny little guy, you sure can eat a lot."

"I'm like a furnace inside. I burn up a lot of fuel." Willie patted his flat little belly.

Back at the cabin, we ate lunch, swam for a while, and stretched out in the sand for our usual mid-day nap. We were all sleeping peacefully.

"Ahoy, the island," someone shouted.

The strange voice startled me awake. I abruptly sat up in the sand. A man in a canoe coming down the river shouted again, "Ahoy, the island. May I come ashore?"

"Sure. Come on in," I answered.

Tone and Willie rubbed their eyes as they, too, sat up. "Who's that?" Tone asked sleepily.

"I don't know, but he's wearing a uniform. Maybe he's a game warden."

Very quickly we put on our shorts. The uniformed man paddled the nose of his canoe up onto our beach.

"Afternoon, fellas. I'm Marion Meyer, the area game warden."

"Afternoon, Mr. Meyer. Nice to meet you. What brings you to our little island?" We thought we should be polite.

"Oh, just out checking the river." He scanned the vicinity and spotted our fishing poles. "You boys doin' any fishing?"

We nodded.

"You do have fishing licenses, don't you?"

"Oh, sure. Ladd and I do. Do you want to see them?" Tone said.

"Yes, I'd like that." Then he turned to Willie. "How about you, young man," he said. "Do you have a license?"

"No, sir. I'm only twelve. I don't need one till I'm sixteen."

"Right you are, son."

Tone ran to the cabin and got our fishing licenses from between the pages of a book. He handed them to Mr. Meyer. The warden examined the papers and gave them back to Tone.

"Okay. Thanks, boys. Oh, by the way... would you know anything about someone fishing with setlines in this area?"

Willie looked questioningly at me with just a little fear in his eyes. "Setlines?" I said. "You mean a bunch of hooks on one line?"

"Yeah, setlines... for catching a lot of fish."

"We've got our poles here, as you can see. We fish with them."

The warden nodded his head. "How about you, little guy? You fish with those poles, too?"

"Yep. And I'm the best fisherman here, too," Willie bragged.

Mr. Meyer chuckled. "I'd bet you probably are. Well, you boys have fun." He got into his canoe, pushed off from the beach and paddled away.

We waited in silence until he was far enough away, not able to hear us.

"I'm the best fisherman here?" I laughed, mocking Willie's remark to the warden. "Willie? You can lie with the best of them."

Willie grinned. "I don't think he believed us one bit. And by the way... talk about lying... you told a good one there, too."

"What do you mean? He asked me if I knew what setlines were, and I told him that I did. Then he asked if someone was using them, and I told him that we used our fishing poles. I didn't tell him that we *didn't* use setlines. *That* would have been a lie."

Willie laughed. "So answering the question just right makes it not a lie. I'm gonna have to remember that one."

"We're gonna have trouble with him before this summer is over," Tone said.

We could bank on that.

Chapter 33

With the game warden hanging around the area, it was better not to put out any more setlines. For the time being, we'd leave the number at four. So we just dug bait and checked lines for the next few days. As long as we didn't have lines with a bunch of hooks in the boat, we took Ahab with us. He wasn't too keen on the idea of going on the water at first, but Willie held him in his lap until the pooch got over his fear. After that he was fascinated when we pulled a fish out of the water dangling on a hook. He'd bark at the fish and make all kinds of racket until we put it in the bucket. Even after we had the fish in the bucket, he'd stick his head in and try to catch them. "Ahab, you'll get stung by one of those cats and you won't be very happy about it," Willie said. The dog just gave Willie a puzzled look, and then stuck his head back into the bucket, terrorizing the catfish.

We had settled into a routine on our island. Get up, have breakfast, dig worms, dig clams, check lines, eat, swim, nap, chop firewood, eat, read, and go to sleep. It was a good life and we enjoyed every minute of it.

Our food supply was running low again, so we decided to check our lines one more time, clean what we caught and those that we had in our pen, and take them into town to trade for groceries. We paddled up to our first line. Tone pulled up about three feet of cord, and that was all that was there. "What the heck?" he said. "Look at this. Someone cut our line."

"Let's check the next one," Willie said. We paddled down river to the next line. It, too, was cut.

"Our good friend, Mr. Meyer. I'll bet he found them!" I said.

When he pulled up only three feet of the third line, Willie said disgustedly, "He found this one too."

The warden hadn't found our newest line between the islands downriver from the cabin. It was still intact, and we had six more nice catfish. Ahab barked at them for a while, and then he decided it wasn't worth the trouble any more. He found a new interest, watching the scenery from the bow of the boat, and he seemed to enjoy having his nose pointed into the breeze.

"How's he finding them? Do you suppose he spots those little strips of cloth?" I asked.

"Didn't you see that big hook he had in his canoe when he was here the other day?" Willie said. "He's got a gigantic treble hook on a long rope. I'll bet he drags that along and snags the lines and then pulls them up and cuts them."

"No, I didn't see that, Willie. But I'll bet you're right," Tone said.

"Well, we've got enough fish to take to town anyway, and I've got an idea how we can fix Mr. Meyer," Willie said with an evil grin.

We cleaned the fish and paddled to town. Ahab came along so Willie could show him off to his mom.

"What a cute puppy! Who's dog is it?" his mom asked.

"He's mine. His name is Ahab. I rescued him from the river in the flood," Willie said proudly.

"Willie! You were in the water in the flood?"

"Relax, ma. I had a rope tied around me. And besides, I couldn't let Ahab just float away and drown! That wouldn't be the Christian thing to do."

His mom shook her head. "Since when does the Christian

thing bother you?"

Willie gave her his most innocent look. She laughed and scratched Ahab's ears. "Well, I guess he can come home with you when you come back, but your sisters will have a fit."

Willie smiled. He hadn't thought of it until just then – now he had a partner in crime for terrorizing his sisters, and together, he and Ahab could wreak havoc on them when the summer was over.

While we were making our usual trade of fish for groceries at Mr. Marcus' store, we remembered that we needed more fishhooks, too, since all but one of our lines had been cut. As we were picking things out I heard Willie ask Mr. Marcus for wire – "Something that isn't too thick, but pretty strong," he said.

"And how much do you need?"

"Oh, maybe fifty feet," Willie replied.

Mr. Marcus went in the back room and came out with a roll of wire. "How about this?" It was thin but strong looking – the kind that was often used for a clothesline.

"Perfect," Willie said.

Tone looked at me and nodded. We knew what he had in mind. "Willie, you're an evil little kid."

Willie grinned. "Mr. Meyer will be sorry he messed with us."

Chapter 34

"**H**e's just the cutest thing I ever saw," Angela said as she held Ahab in her lap, petting his head. Willie rolled his eyes and grinned.

We had stopped at my house and spent some time with my mom, too, and I traded *Moby Dick* for *Huckleberry Finn*, a book that I thought Willie would really like. And now Tone's mom was making quite a fuss over Ahab. We could easily see that Willie was especially proud of his new friend.

"Too bad your dads are away working. I'm sure they'd like to see Ahab, too."

When we mentioned that it was time we should be leaving for the island, Angela insisted that we stay a little longer and have some lunch. So we did.

As usual, we were, once again, heavily loaded down with groceries, canned goods, and plenty of fresh bread when we returned to the boat. "These trips to town sure are worthwhile," I said. "Maybe we should come more often."

"Naw, then we'd just eat too much and get fat and lazy," Tone joked.

When we were well on our way down the river, Tone's curiosity peaked. "So Willie, tell us about your plan with the wire."

"Well, I figure it's no use making new lines till Mr. Meyer leaves us alone," Willie began. "So what I think we should do is just take a piece of cord and tie it off like we do when we put out a setline, and put a strip of cloth on it so it looks just like all the rest of them."

Tone and I stopped paddling and let *Voyageur* drift on the current so we could listen better. This was beginning to sound interesting already.

"I think what Mr. Meyer does," Willie went on, "is float along with that hook dragging behind, and when it snags our lines, he pulls them up and cuts them off. I figure he must either tie the

126

hook to his canoe or to himself, since he can't paddle and hold it."

So far, Tone and I were in total agreement with Willie's theory, and it was plain to see that he had put some thought into his plan.

"So what we'll do is make him think he's going to snag our line, but twenty feet or so above the fake line, we'll stretch our wire across the river, under water, and anchor it to two good solid trees. He'll be waiting to catch our line, but he'll get a big surprise when he snags that wire."

I looked at Tone and we burst out laughing. "Willie, remind me never to get you mad at me," I said.

We took our food back to the cabin and stored it away, and then went out to look for a place to ambush Mr. Meyer. For Willie's plan to work, we needed a narrow channel where there was a fast current. After some searching, we found the perfect spot – a wooded island just forty feet from the riverbank and a rushing current between.

We rigged our fake line and cloth strip onto a root and moved upstream about ten yards. A small tree that had tipped over into the water made the perfect anchor for the wire on the riverbank. Tone leaned over the end of the boat and secured the wire under the surface of the water so it couldn't be seen.

Directly across the channel stood a big tree on the island with heavy roots that went down into the water. We beached the boat, waded in, and stretched the wire as tight as we could get it, wrapping it securely around the big root under the water surface.

"That'll get him," Willie snickered.

We hid the boat in the weeds on the other side of the island and then built a blind with brush and grass so we could hide and watch the fun. We cleared out the leaves and sticks, smoothed out the sand and settled in to wait. We'd seen Mr. Meyer paddle past our island about the same time almost every day for the past week or more, so we knew he'd probably be along within a few hours.

"I'll watch if you guys want to take a nap," Tone said.

It *was* siesta time anyway, so Willie and I lay in the sand and napped. Later I woke up and traded places with Tone so he could get a little shut-eye, too. Willie and Ahab were still fast asleep, snuggled together in the warm sand. That dog had quickly learned our routine.

I was watching a beaver chewing on a sapling on the riverbank. Suddenly the beaver took off running toward the swampy lowland just beyond. Something had scared it. I looked upriver and there came Mr. Meyer in his canoe, right on schedule.

"Guys, wake up! Here he comes," I whispered as I shook Tone and Willie awake.

They sat up and yawned, and Ahab trotted over to a bush and peed on it.

"Ahab! Come," Willie whispered. Ahab trotted back and sat at his master's side.

Mr. Meyer was casually paddling along when he spotted the strip of cloth on the root up ahead. His canoe moved much faster as it was drawn into the swift current of the channel when he tossed the rope with the big treble hook into the water behind him. He slipped the loop tied in the other end of the rope over his shoulder and around his neck.

"I hope it doesn't break his neck," I whispered.

Willie giggled.

The warden smiled and began paddling faster. He dug the paddle into the river and made a couple of hard strokes and was moving along quite fast. He was just about even with the flag when the hook snagged the submerged wire. The rope tightened with a "*Twang*" and jerked Mr. Meyer backwards over the end of the canoe faster than you would imagine it could happen. The canoe and the warden's hat floated down the river, while Mr. Meyer struggled to keep his head above water. Tone started to stand up. I stopped him. "Just wait. He'll probably get loose," I said.

"We don't want to drown him," Tone whispered.

A few seconds later, Mr. Meyer popped up to the surface and

swam toward the riverbank. He had slipped the rope off his shoulder and left his big treble hook on the bottom of the river. He climbed up onto dry land, a dreadful sight, standing there in his drenched uniform. He saw his canoe floating away and immediately began running through the brush and briars chasing after it. But by that time, the canoe was already at least a hundred yards down river.

"The mosquitoes will have a feast on him if he keeps thrashing through that brush and grass," Willie giggled.

Not only were there thousands of mosquitoes, but there was prickly ash and lots of poison ivy growing on that riverbank.

We probably should have been feeling a little guilty about our prank and the added trouble we caused the warden – losing his canoe, and all. We hadn't really planned on that happening. But we all laughed anyway, as Mr. Meyer got farther and farther down the riverbank chasing his canoe. In a short time, we couldn't hear him crashing through the brush any more.

"I don't think he'll be bothering us for a while," Tone said.

We slid Voyageur back into the water, retrieved the wire and rolled it up. We would save it just in case we needed it again some day.

"Well, what do ya think?" Willie beamed. "S'pose we can make some more setlines now. I think Mr. Meyer will probably pester somebody else for the rest of the summer."

Tone slapped Willie on the back. "Willie, you did good."

Willie hugged Ahab. "Hear that, Ahab? I did good."

Chapter 35

That evening we celebrated with some sausages cooked over the fire pit and a whole apple pie that Tone's mom had sent with us.

"No sense in letting it get stale," Willie laughed as he popped the last bite of pie into his mouth. Ahab was sitting right next to him in the sand and had been getting handouts from all of us. When the last bite disappeared, he looked a little disappointed, but he lay down with his head on Willie's lap, closed his eyes and soon was snoring.

"He sounds like you Ladd," Willie said.

"I don't snore, do I?"

"Like a grizzly bear," Tone remarked.

"Like a whole cabin full of grizzlies," Willie laughed.

"Well it's better than those fart noises that come from your end of the hammock," I said to Willie.

"You're just jealous," he said raising his leg.

"Don't! You'll kill poor little Ahab," I joked as I ducked for cover.

We all had a good laugh and then Willie said, "How about reading some more of *A Tale of Two Cities*?"

I got the book and one of the lamps from the cabin, lay back in the warm sand and began reading. Willie rolled over on his side so he could watch me read. Tone leaned back against a log and closed his eyes. I read for over two hours and came to the end of the story:

"It is a far far better thing that I do, then I have ever done, it is a far far better rest that I go to than I have ever known. The End."

"Wow! What a good story, Ladd. You sure read good. I can almost see all of that stuff happening when you say it," Willie said.

"I've listened to Ladd read since we were little kids, Willie, and he always makes it like that."

"But you're a good reader, too, Tone," I said.

"Yeah, I can read, but not like you do. I just read. You make it real."

And with that said, we picked up our stuff, woke Ahab, and went to the cabin to sleep.

Although we weren't keeping track of time or the number of days that we were on the island, we knew that it had to be near the end of June, or maybe into the early part of July. The days passed uneventfully, but each one was a treasure. We had plenty to eat, the weather was perfect, and we had each other's great companionship.

The river was getting low as it always did in the summer, so we had to be more careful where we went in the boat as not to get stranded on a sandbar.

"This is what they must have been talking about when Father Marquette and Joliet explored the Wisconsin." I said.

"What are you talking about?" Willie asked.

To the best of my recollection, I recited a little history for Willie: "The Wisconsin river was explored in 1673 by a Jesuit priest and a French mapmaker who were trying to find a passage to the Pacific Ocean, and thought that the Wisconsin might flow into it. They paddled up the coast of Lake Michigan, and up the Fox River, and then crossed land and started down the Wisconsin. The local Indians called it "The Stream of a Thousand Islands." They had two big birch bark canoes and five other men with them, and probably came right past this island over two hundred years ago."

"Wow, that's neat to imagine," Willie said.

"I read about it a few years ago," I said. "Father Marquette wrote: *"It is very wide; it has a sandy bottom, which forms various shoals that render it's navigation very difficult. On the banks one sees fertile land, diversified with woods, prairies and hills."*

"It sounds like he was talking about right here," Tone commented.

"They probably paddled right past here. Just imagine paddling a canoe over four hundred miles in a place that no one knew anything about. Those guys were pretty brave."

"Wouldn't that be a trip?"

"What do you mean?"

"If we could get up to the start of the Wisconsin, we could float *our* boat all the way back down here, just like the Voyageurs did," Willie said.

"Our only problem would be getting four hundred miles *upriver*," I said.

But it was something worth dreaming about.

Chapter 36

It was probably safe to put out setlines again, now that we had discouraged Mr. Meyer from spending too much time on *our* side of the river. We had made up some new lines and were ready to go back into business again, but first we needed clams for bait. So we paddled up to the clam bed, beached *Voyageur* on the sand bar, and started digging through the sand with our feet. I heard a clunking noise upriver; two men were rowing toward us in a sorry looking old flat bottom boat.

"Who do you suppose *they* are?" I whispered, and nodded my head upriver toward the men.

"Look like bums," Tone whispered.

The men rowed their boat up next to *Voyageur* and climbed out onto the sandbar. The one at the front of the old scow was bald except for a ring of hair grown out about five inches long right around the bottom of his skull. His head looked like a big egg sitting on a nest of brown grass. His shirt and overalls were tattered and dirty, and the work boots on his feet looked as though they should have been thrown out years ago. The younger man at the back of the boat was pretty heavy set with stringy red hair, most of his teeth missing, shirtless and barefoot. Both looked like they hadn't bathed in weeks.

"What you guys looking for?" Baldy said.

"We're hunting clams... for bait," Willie answered.

"Catchin' a lot of fish?" Baldy asked.

"We get a few now and then," I said. While we were talking to Baldy, I noticed that Red was looking our boat over pretty carefully.

"Nice boat you got here. Wanna trade?" he said laughing.

We stared at the leaky old sieve they called a boat and grinned. "Don't think so, but thanks anyway," Tone said.

"You guys don't got any extra food, do ya?" Red asked.

"Not with us," Willie said.

I shot Willie a quick warning glance, and he realized I didn't want him to volunteer any more information.

"Where are you guys heading?" I asked.

"We hear tell there's jobs in Prairie du Chien working on the riverboats. Gonna row down there and see if we can get some work," Red said.

"Well, hope you have some luck finding a job," Tone said, and began wading again, looking for clams.

The two men must have taken that as a hint that we had other stuff to do besides talking to them. Baldy climbed back into their boat, Red pushed them off and jumped in. The only other things in the boat with them were a knapsack, a couple of filthy old blankets, and about three inches of dirty water sloshing around in the bottom.

"Good luck with your fishing," Red called out as they slid away on the current.

We waved goodbye, glad to be rid of the visitors. When they were out of earshot, I said in a low voice to Tone, "Good thing we were here with the boat or they would have had it and been gone." Tone nodded in agreement.

We worked our way down the river baiting and putting out our newly made lines. It took us a couple of hours, and by the time we got back to the island we were pretty hungry. Willie jumped out onto the sand and trotted up to the cabin. Tone and I pulled the boat up onto the beach, and Ahab ran for a tree.

"Ladd! Tone! We've been robbed!" Willie came running from the cabin. "All our stuff is gone!"

"What? Everything?"

"Everything 'cept the stove. It had to be those bums."

Tone and I dashed to the cabin and it was as empty as the day we finished building it. The cooler was open and emptied. The hammocks were gone; the lanterns, our blankets and pillows; all the pots and pans – gone. Everything was gone except our books.

Tone grabbed *David Copperfield* and let out a sigh of relief. Our fishing licenses and three dollars were still hidden between the pages. "Well, they probably can't read anyway, or they'd have taken this too," he said.

"What are we gonna do now?" Willie cried.

"We're gonna get our stuff back," Tone said with determination. "We just gotta think about this first – not go off half cocked."

"You're right." I added. "We need to figure out a plan."

After a long moment of thought Tone said, "They have that old leaky boat, so they won't get far with all that stuff in it. They'll probably pull up on an island someplace downriver and camp for the night. We can catch up to them pretty easily. We'll just have to be careful to see them before they see us."

"What then?"

"Then we'll wait till it gets dark and get our stuff back."

Willie broke a dead branch from a tree and swung it like a baseball bat. "I'm gonna crack their skulls if they give us any trouble."

Tone and I broke out laughing. "Jeez, Willie! Remind me not to piss you off," I said.

Willie grinned and swung his club again.

We pushed off from the island and began paddling down river, watching for our thieves. Voyageur slid through the water so easily that we knew we could catch up to them in their leaky old boat, so we took our time and made sure to keep out of sight.

The sun was getting low in the sky when Willie suddenly pointed ahead and said, "There they are!" A column of smoke rising from an island about two hundred yards ahead gave away their position. We knew it had to be them – they hadn't bothered to hide that old wreck of a flat bottom boat, and we could just barely make out Baldy and Red sitting by the fire.

"Those dirty turds. They're eating our food," Willie said. "And I'm hungry as heck."

"Just be patient," I told Willie. We'll wait for it to get dark, and then we'll sneak in there and get our stuff."

We pulled up on the opposite side of another island just above them, and snuck through the brush and grass until we could see them without getting out in the open. They were only about fifty yards away. Tone crawled over behind a thick tree and stood up so he could get a better look at the river between us and the other island. He crawled back. "It's sandbar all the way across. Looks like it's only a foot or so deep. We can wade across and get our stuff when they go to sleep."

We could smell our food cooking, and watched Red and Baldy eat like pigs. Ahab began whining, as he smelled the food, too. "Shhhhhh, Ahab. Be quiet. We'll eat later," Willie whispered.

When they had finished eating, Red got what appeared to be a bottle of wine out of the sack in the bottom of the boat. They opened it and began passing it back and forth, laughing and having a great time, obviously quite proud of themselves for their dirty deed.

Daylight faded away. Willie and Ahab were curled up in the sand, snoring. Tone and I watched and listened as the wine started to take its affect on Baldy and Red. "Drink up, boys," I said. "All the easier to get our stuff back."

The moon was just rising when the two crooks climbed into our hammocks tied between some trees. We waited a half hour to make sure they were sleeping soundly, and then woke Willie. "Let's go, they're sleeping, and they're drunk."

Willie nodded and told Ahab to stay. Ahab whined a little, but stayed put. We slowly waded across to the other island, careful not to lift our feet out of the water to keep from making any splashing noise, and then quietly snuck to the crooks' campsite. We could hear them snoring, so we knew they hadn't noticed us coming. We began gathering up our stuff, and soon had everything except the hammocks.

"Let's take this back and get our boat," I whispered. "We can come back and try to get the hammocks."

Tone and Willie nodded, and we slowly crept back across the shallow water. Ahab was overjoyed to see us and began jumping up and down. Willie quieted him down and we put our stuff in the boat.

"We'll beach our boat on the other side of the island where the water is deeper," I explained my plan. "Then one of us can sneak around and push their boat into the current. We'll make a bunch of noise and wake them up. When they go after their boat, we'll cut down the hammocks and get the heck out of there." Tone thought the plan would work, and Willie grinned evilly.

We carefully paddled to the other side of the island and pulled *Voyageur* up on the sand. Baldy and Red were still sleeping peacefully.

"I'll go and push their boat off," Willie whispered.

Tone and I, each with our Swiss Army knives out and ready for action, snuck into the trees close to the sleeping thieves. Baldy was snoring like a hibernating bear. Willie snuck past them and gave their old boat a shove into the river. Then he did something totally unexpected: he picked up a piece of a burned off log and smacked Baldy in the butt. "You're boat's floating away!"

Baldy jumped up and fell out of the hammock. He stumbled to his feet and staggered toward the edge of the water. In the moonlight, he saw their leaky old flat bottom drifting away. "Git up! Git up, John!" he screamed. "Our boat's gittin' away!"

With a confused stare, Red sat up. Just as he did, Willie smacked him in the knee with the log.

"Hey! That kid is here!" Baldy yelled. "Get him! He let our boat go!"

Willie scampered away and Red lumbered after him, limping on his right knee. Baldy was up to his waist in the water trying to catch the boat. It only took seconds for Tone and I to cut the hammock cords, grab them and run for the boat. "Willie! Come on, we've got 'em!" I shouted.

Willie dodged back and forth eluding Red and stopped just a second too long when he heard me yell. Red grabbed him by the strap of his bibs and pulled him to the ground.

"Now, you little shit. We're gonna get our stuff back or you're gonna get a beatin'!" He lifted his hand to slap Willie when Ahab

137

launched himself off the sand and clamped his jaws onto Red's left butt cheek. He growled ferociously, shaking his head. Red let out a yell that would have woke up the dead. "Yieeee! I'm bit! I'm bit!"

Red forgot about Willie and let him go. Willie scrambled to his feet and ran toward Tone and me. "Ahab, come on!" he shouted. Ahab let loose of his victim and came running to Willie. He still had a piece of Red's overalls in his teeth. We all jumped into *Voyageur* and Tone and I began paddling as fast as we could up the river.

Willie laughed like crazy as he took the piece of Red's trousers from Ahab. "Good boy, Ahab. Good boy."

As we paddled away, we could hear Baldy and Red cussing and shouting. It seems their boat got away and they couldn't catch up to it. We weren't sure how well they could swim, but if they couldn't, they were going to be stranded for a while. It couldn't happen to a couple of nicer guys.

We paddled for a couple of hours to finally get home to our island. "Let's leave everything except the hammocks and blankets and pillows," I suggested. "Let's just go to bed. I'm dead tired."

Nobody argued. We pulled *Voyageur* up onto the sand and went to the cabin. In just a few minutes, the hammocks were hung, and we were in them. We were hungry and still kind of excited from the encounter with Baldy and Red, but it didn't take long for all of us to fall asleep.

When all was said and done, we had only lost a bunch of food. Baldy and Red must have been pretty darn hungry because they ate enough of our food to feed a small army. We had plenty of store credit with Mr. Marcus, so we made a trip to town to replenish our stock.

We never heard any more about Baldy and Red, and they never showed up near us again. They were probably afraid of our vicious guard dog.

Chapter 37

Sitting by the fire the next night, I had just started reading *Huckleberry Finn:*

"You don't know about me without you have read a book by the name of The Adventures of Tom Sawyer; but that ain't no matter."

"Have you read *Tom Sawyer,* Willie?" I asked.

"Yeah, we read it in school last year. It was good, except Tom liked that girl, Becky. Yuck."

"You don't like girls?" Tone asked.

"I've got four sisters! What do you think?"

"Your oldest sisters, Ellie and Frannie are pretty cute," I said.

"Oh God! I'm gonna be sick!" Willie clutched his belly and fell over in the sand.

"Just you wait, Willie," Tone said. "One of these days girls won't look so bad to you. You'll see."

Willie stuck his finger in his mouth and pretended to throw up.

Just then a rocket streaked through the air and exploded over town. "What the heck was that?" Willie asked.

"It must be the Fourth of July," Tone replied. A second rocket exploded in a bright flash of red and blue.

For the next hour we watched as rockets burst and colored the sky. The noise scared Ahab, but Willie held him tight to make him feel safe.

"Well, at least we know what day it is," I said. After the fireworks show, I read for a while longer, and then we went to bed.

We had good luck with the setlines during the next two weeks, and went to town three times with pails of fresh fish. We were catching fish faster than we could eat up the profits, so we built up a sizeable credit with Mr. Marcus.

During those two weeks, it was so hot that we did most of our cooking over the campfire at the beach. We got in the habit of checking our setlines first thing in the morning when it was cooler, and then fished and swam, but mostly just took it easy during the day when it got too hot.

On our third trip to town, we stopped to see Mr. DeSilva because we hadn't heard from him in quite a while. He said that he had received a letter from Mr. Honer saying that he'd be delivering a load of caskets sometime during the third week of July.

"Just send Ronnie down and we'll come and help you," Tone and I said.

About a week later, Ronnie appeared on the riverbank late one morning. "Hey, guys! Mr. DeSilva wants you to come and unload caskets for him."

"Okay... thanks Ronnie. You want to ride back with us or stay here with Willie?"

"I'll come over and stay there for the day," he said. "I already told my Ma and she said I can stay." He stripped off his clothes, held them over his head with one hand and side stroked across the channel.

"Jeez, Ronnie. You swim like a fish," Willie said.

Ronnie tossed his clothes on the sand. "Let's take a swim, Willie."

The two kids were in the water splashing, and Ahab was making a big fuss as we slid the boat into the water and paddled away. "You guys be careful and don't do anything stupid," I said.

"Yes, mom!" they both yelled back and began laughing hilariously.

"What a couple of characters," Tone said. "Were we ever that obnoxious when we were that age?"

"Who? Us?"

Chapter 38

W e pulled the boat up on the riverbank and walked into town to the Funeral Home. Mr. DeSilva and Mr. Honer were sitting under a big maple tree sipping lemonade.

"Ah. Here comes our natives now," said Mr. DeSilva.

"Have you native boys seen Tone and Ladd?" Mr. Honer chuckled.

"Hi, Mr. Honer," I said, shaking his hand.

"Hi, sir," Tone said. He shook hands with the big man."

"Please call me Harvey, boys. Not *Mr.* Honer, not *sir.* Just plain old Harvey.

We nodded in acknowledgement.

"My! The summer seems to have been good for you. You both look quite fit and tan, and you look like you've been feeding well."

"We have, Harvey. Our cabin turned out just great, the boat is the best ever, and we've just had a great time. By the way... thanks much for those paddles. They work just perfect."

"I thought they'd be something you could put to good use."

"Willie from next door is staying with us, too. He's such a neat kid, and we invited him to spend the summer with us.

Mr. Honer smiled his approval.

"You should see him. He's all brown; his hair is as long as a girl and it's bleached out blonde as one of his sisters. He's really a funny kid."

"So it's been good. That's great, boys. And I'm glad you took in young Willie. He needs some happiness in his life; he's had a hard time of it growing up. Everything has gone as planned, then?"

"Well, we did have a flood, and a little trouble with the game warden, and a couple of bums tried to steal all our stuff, but nothing serious. We even rescued a little dog floating on a log jam during the flood, and now he's Willie's best friend."

"I'm real happy for you. Now, how about if you two unload those caskets while Mr. DeSilva and I go up to the hotel and wash the dust from our throats?" Harvey said with a twinkle in his eye.

"Happy to, Harvey. Same as usual, Mr. DeSilva? One in the viewing room and the extras in the garage?"

"Yes. All but those two in the front. Harvey's taking them down to Lancaster. Special order for some rich family."

"So, you're not going back right away?" I said to Harvey.

"I'm staying here tonight, and then tomorrow I'll drive to Lancaster. I'm hoping I can get there in a day, and a day coming back. Then it's about a week to get home."

"Okay. Well, we'll get right to work, and you two go and have a cold one," Tone said grinning.

"Or two." Harvey said laughing uproariously at his own joke.

While we unloaded the caskets, Tone and I began talking about the idea of taking a trip down the river like Father Marquette had done. Ever since we had mentioned it that day out on the island, the idea had been brewing.

"Harvey lives in Wausau. That's probably about two hundred miles up river from here," I said. "How long do you suppose it would take us to paddle back from up there?"

"I'd think we could paddle twenty miles a day, or maybe more." Tone thought a long moment. "Do you think we could do it?"

"Harvey's wagon will be empty, and I'd bet he would give us a lift to Wausau."

Our excitement rose the more we talked about it. "We've got enough money saved... we can buy food along the way, and we can catch fish to eat some days if we're not near a town."

"What about Willie?" Tone asked. "Do you think his mom would let him go?"

"He'd never go without Ahab. I don't know, but we'll cross that bridge when we come to it."

We finished unloading the caskets, set one of each in the showroom, cleaned up all the packing material, smashed the crates and lit them on fire. Like clockwork, Mr. DeSilva and Harvey came walking down the street just as we were done.

"Perfect timing," Harvey said. "The work seems to be all finished." He laughed and slapped his thigh with his big hand.

"Harvey, we'd like to ask you something," I said.

"Ask away, boys."

"We've been talking about a great adventure to trace the journey of the Voyageurs – Father Marquette and Pierre Joliet – down the Wisconsin River."

Harvey appeared a little curious.

"We wondered if you might give us a ride to Wausau when you go back," Tone said. "We'd take our boat along and then paddle back here, like the explorers did. What do you think?"

Harvey rubbed his chin during a brief thought. "Boys, I'd be more than happy to give you a ride. I'd enjoy the company of two such fine lads as you any time."

"Willie and Ahab might come, too," I said. "Would that be okay?"

"Who's Ahab?"

"Willie's dog. The one we rescued in the flood."

"Kind of a strange name for a dog, isn't it?"

"He got the name from *Moby Dick*. I've been reading the classics to him and Tone almost every evening by the fire."

"So young Willie is getting a little education during this adventure, too. That's admirable, boys. Sure, you can all come along. I'd be happy to have you."

"What if one of our fine citizens happens to drop dead while you're on this quest?" Mr. DeSilva asked.

"We'll find someone to take our place before we leave," I said. "Just don't give our jobs to anyone permanently."

"Don't worry about that, boys. You'll have a job as long as you want it. Just let me know who to contact in case we need a hole."

"I'll meet you here in three days," Harvey said.

Mr. DeSilva paid us and we headed over to my house to discuss our plans with my mom. When we arrived, both Moms were sipping lemonade at the picnic table in our yard. We were glad that we only had to explain the plans for our trip once.

143

"Just how long will this expedition take?" my mom asked.

"And what about school?" Angela added.

"Mr. Honer says it takes about a week to get to Wausau, and we figure about two weeks to come back by boat. So you see? We'll be back in plenty of time for school."

"Well," Angela said. "I guess it would be okay with me." She glanced at my mom.

"Yes, it would be quite an experience for you, but you'd better go discuss this with your dads, first," my mom said. "They're at a worksite over on the east side of town today."

Once we had the moms' approval, contingent on what our dads would say, we headed to the east side.

They were just starting a new house. Dad was helping Robert lay out the trenches for the foundation, so Robert could begin the masonry work while Dad worked on the house he was building where we tore down the summer kitchen.

Again, we explained our plans. "It's okay with our moms," I said. "They said to talk to you."

"Well, Eric," Tone's dad said. "It sure would be one heck of a test of our boat building skills."

"It would, in deed," Dad replied. "That's a mighty long trip, boys. Think you're up to it?"

"Sure, we are! We've survived the summer on our own, so far, haven't we?"

"You have, at that. Guess I don't have any objections. How 'bout you, Robert."

"None that I can think of. Just be careful."

"Thanks Dad," Tone and I blurted out, almost in unison.

We couldn't say anything to Willie about the trip until we knew his mom would let him go. It would be quite a disappointment for him if he got his hopes up, and then she didn't approve. So we headed over to Willie's house to talk to his mom next.

Chapter 39

W e could hear a lot of laughter and chatter as we walked up to the back door at Willie's house. Willie's sisters were setting the table for supper, and we could see his mom through the kitchen window. Tone knocked.

Willie's mom looked up from rolling out a piecrust. "The door's open," she said, and motioned for us to come in.

When we walked in and she realized Willie wasn't with us, she stopped rolling and a worried stare came on her face. "Has something happened to Willie?" She motioned for us to sit down.

"Oh, no. He's just fine," I said. "We came into town to help Mr. DeSilva unload caskets today, so Willie and Ronnie are at the cabin fishing."

That brought a sigh of relief to Willie's mom.

"We wanted to ask you about something concerning Willie, though," Tone said as he sat down at the kitchen table.

"Oh? What is it?" she asked, as if she suspected Willie might be causing us some trouble.

"Well," Tone began. "We've been reading about the Voyageurs, Father Marquette and Pierre Joliet, and how they explored the Wisconsin River. Ladd reads almost every night to Willie and me before we go to bed, and he read about their adventures. Anyway, Mr. Honer, the man who builds the caskets lives at Wausau. We asked him if we could hitch a ride with him back to Wausau in a couple of days, and then we'll paddle our boat back here, kind of like the Voyageurs did a couple of hundred years ago."

"And we'd like Willie to come with us," I added.

"Willie's not being any trouble?"

"Not at all. He's a good kid. We really like him and enjoy having him there with us," Tone said.

"Are you sure you're talking about *my* Willie?"

We laughed. "Yes, *your* Willie," I said.

"I think Willie is real happy to have some other boys to hang around with," Tone said. "He kind of thinks of Ladd and me as his big brothers. We think of him as our little brother, too."

His mom smiled. "He's had a hard time. When his daddy died, Willie was left here alone with all these women, and I must say that my girls love to torment him. I'm glad he's made friends with you boys; I guess he does need someone besides girls around him all the time." She paused a few moments in thought. "You'll take good care of him, won't you?"

"We'll take *real* good care of him," I said. "Just like he was our *real* little brother."

"How long will you be gone?" There was still just a twinge of reluctance in her voice.

"We figure to be on the river about two weeks, and that will get us home in plenty of time before school starts again."

"Well, okay," she finally gave in. "Take him along and let him see some of the rest of the world. I'll send some canned meat with you, and I just baked cookies. You can take some of them, too."

Willie's two oldest sisters, Ellie and Frannie, came into the kitchen while his mom was gathering up the food. They were admiring our suntans and how strong we looked without our shirts. Just as Frannie was squeezing Tone's bicep, Willie's mother came back into the kitchen and shooed them away. "Just what I need. My girls flirting with boys," she said smiling. "But if they must flirt, I guess I'd be happy if it was with good looking boys like you." Tone and I blushed.

While Willie's mom boxed up the food for us, Tone and I each had a glass of milk and a couple of cookies. "Does Willie need anything?" she asked.

"I don't think so. He's got his bib overalls, and that's all he ever wears anyway," I said.

"I swear that boy would run naked all summer if I'd let him," she said laughing.

We thanked her for the cookies and milk and the other food and started toward the river. We had only gone part of a block when Ellie and Frannie caught up with us. They asked if they could walk us to the river. Ellie slipped her arm into mine, and Frannie did the same with Tone. On the way, we told them about our trip to Wausau, and they suggested that we leave Willie there if we could. We bid them farewell and they stood on the riverbank, waving as we paddled away.

"Maybe going back to school isn't going to be so bad after all," Tone said as he waved to the girls.

Chapter 40

When Tone and I got back to the island, Willie and Ronnie were fishing from the sand beach. They waved as we came into view and Willie held up a stringer with several nice catfish. "We caught supper!" he shouted.

"Let's wait till Ronnie goes home to tell Willie about the trip," I said, "I don't want him to feel left out."

Tone agreed. We pulled the boat up on the sand and joined the two kids. "Well, what did you guys do all day?" I asked.

"We had a lot of fun," Ronnie said. "We swam, and fished, and ate, and played catch with Ahab. And we took a nap in the sand."

Willie nodded in agreement.

"Well, I s'pose I better be heading back home," Ronnie said as he gathered up his clothes. "I sure had fun today."

"Jump in the boat," Tone said to Ronnie. "I'll give you a lift to shore."

Tone paddled him across, gave Ronnie a quarter and thanked him for bringing the message about Mr. Honer needing our help.

"See ya later," Ronnie told Tone, and then he shouted across to Willie and me, "See ya, guys."

We waved to Ronnie. Willie said, "I'll go start some potatoes?"

"Just wait a few minutes," I said. "Tone and I have something to talk to you about."

Willie got a worried look on his face.

"Don't worry, Willie," I assured him. "It's nothing bad."

A couple of minutes later, Tone joined us, and we all sat in the sand with our feet in the water. "Willie, remember when I told you about the Voyageurs?"

"Sure. Father Marquette and Pierre somebody. They discovered the Wisconsin river."

"Right. Well we talked to Mr. Honer today, about hitching a ride back to Wausau with him, and then paddling our boat down the river till we get home. It won't be the whole river, but it'll be a lot of it. We thought it would make a good adventure for the end of the summer."

Willie frowned with disappointed. "I see. When are you leaving?"

"Mr. Honer has to deliver some caskets to Lancaster, and he'll be back in two days. We'll be leaving the next day," Tone said.

Willie nodded. "Well, I guess that will be a fun trip for you."

"Us, Willie."

He didn't get it at first. "What do you mean?"

"We talked to your mom, already. She said it'd be all right for you to come along."

Willie's eyes got as big as saucers. "I get to go along? No foolin'? You wouldn't fool with me, would you?" He grabbed me by the shoulders and looked me straight in the eyes. "No foolin'?"

"No foolin,' Willie. You can go with us, unless you'd rather go back home and spend some time with your sisters before school starts."

"Arrrgggghhh!" Willie clutched his heart and flopped over onto the sand. Then he jumped to his feet, ran to the end of the sandbar and did a flip into the river. He came up to the surface and began splashing and yelling and going a little nuts. Tone looked at me and grinned. "I guess we can take it that he *does* want to go."

All through supper and afterward when we were talking about the trip, we couldn't keep Willie still for a minute. As we planned our supplies and how we would make a shelter, he paced back and forth. It was hard to get to sleep that nigh after all the excitement. As I turned out the lamp, I heard Willie whisper to Ahab, "We're going on a big trip boy. Won't that be fun?" Ahab licked Willie's face and snuggled down next to him in the hammock.

Chapter 41

During the next two days we worked hard figuring out what we needed to take with us. We wanted all the essentials without being too overloaded. After we pulled up all of our setlines, rolled them up on pieces of cut off planks and stored them away, we started to gather our gear.

Our list included just the basics: blankets, a few pots and pans, three tin pie pans to eat from, and some of the canned meat. The fishing gear was essential, as that would provide many of our meals, and Tone's hatchet for cutting firewood. We didn't need much for clothes – just an extra pair of shorts, one shirt and some extra underwear for each. Of course, Willie had his ever-present bib overall shorts. We hadn't seen Willie wear shoes all summer, so there was no point in asking him if he needed any with him on the trip, and Tone and I decided we really didn't need any shoes either – we'd be on the river all the time.

We experimented with a shelter for sleeping on the islands and sandbars in the river. We found that if we tipped the boat on its side and put a paddle under each end, it would stand up and would provide one side of a shelter. A canvas tarp draped over the boat and paddles completed our shelter. It looked somewhat like a tent and would be just the thing for the journey. On warm, dry nights, we could roll up the tarp so we had fresh air, and on cooler nights, or if it rained, we could put it all the way down and we'd be snug inside.

"I'm gonna miss this place," Willie said sadly as we pushed off from our beach early on the morning we were to meet Harvey.

"We'll come back here," I said as I paddled against the current. "We'll come here when we get back from our trip, and we can camp here on weekends even after school starts."

"Yeah, we could come even in cool weather," Willie said. "The stove will keep us warm no matter how cold it gets." He seemed a little more at ease about leaving once he knew that our time at our island cabin wasn't completely over.

We paddled to our usual spot on the riverbank near town. Mr. Honer and Ronnie were already there waiting for us.

"Hey, lads!" Mr. Honer shouted just before we nosed onto the beach. "All ready for your great adventure?"

"All ready, Harvey," I answered.

"You going too, Willie?" Ronnie asked.

"Yep. Me and Ahab, too," Willie said with a big grin.

Ahab jumped and pranced in the boat and gave a few little barks, as if he knew there was something wonderful in store for him.

Ronnie and Harvey helped us load *Voyageur* and the rest of the gear onto his big wagon. We bid Ronnie farewell and off we went down the road to begin the greatest adventure we had ever known.

I rode up on the wagon seat with Harvey, and Tone and Willie rode in the back for the first two or three hours. When we stopped to water the horses, Tone and I switched places. Later Willie sat with Harvey and we could hear him telling about all the big fish we had caught and the story of the big flood. Harvey laughed non-stop at Willie's tall tales. It was quite a sight to see a big man like Harvey sitting next to little Willie laughing and smiling, as if they were made for each other.

Arriving at the village of Spring Green late that afternoon, Harvey pulled the wagon up in front of the livery stable. He went inside and made arrangements for the horses to be fed and bedded down, and for the wagon with our boat and gear to be stored inside the barn where it would be safe.

"Well, Harvey, we'll see you in the morning," Willie said.

"We'll bed down in the wagon, and we've got some food along for supper," I added.

"Now that's not necessary, boys. We'll stay at the hotel where we can get a soft bed and a good meal."

Tone and I exchanged worried glances. We had intended to use our money for food on the trip, but we knew what we had wouldn't be enough to last if we were to pay for a hotel room each night on the way upriver.

"Harvey, we'd better just sleep in the wagon," I said. "We don't have enough money to spend on a hotel room."

"The rooms are on me, and so are the meals."

"Oh, but we can't ask you to spend that much money on us," I said.

"You didn't ask. I offered. Listen boys, I do well with my business. There's always a guaranteed customer." He laughed. "People die every day just to be buried in my caskets. I take some lumber, and sometimes brass or tin, and have some very talented employees make that lumber and tin into a very expensive box. I make good money on them."

We all listened intently as Harvey sighed and went on. "I have no family of my own anymore. My wife died and my only son was killed in a fire. I enjoy every one of my trips to Muscoda because I look forward to seeing you boys. You're bright, polite and good helpers. And if you will permit an old man to do so, I'd like to treat you to some meals and a bed while we are on the road."

"You're a real nice man, Harvey," Tone said, offering his hand. "Thank you, very much." Then I shook Harvey's hand and Willie gave him a hug. Harvey's eyes got a little teary.

"What about Ahab?" Willie asked.

"We'll leave him here with the stableman for now, and after we eat supper we'll sneak him into the hotel with us," Harvey said with a conspiratorial wink.

As we walked toward the hotel, Harvey put his arm on Willie's shoulder and said, "You know, young Willie, my son was just about one year older than you when he died, and he looked a lot like you – blonde hair, green eyes, big smile."

Willie's white teeth sparkled when he gave Harvey one of his smiles that were even more dazzling than usual, now that he was so tan. Then a serious look came to his face. "I'm sorry about your son, Harvey. Anytime you need a hug, I've got one for you."

"I'll keep that in mind, Willie. I surely will."

Chapter 42

"**B**etter bring your shirts along, boys. I don't think they'll let you eat in the dining room without them."

"We didn't bring any shoes. Is that gonna be okay?" Tone asked.

"I don't think they'll worry about that. I've seen lots of barefoot youngsters in the hotels. And they like the money I spend a lot more than any rules about bare feet."

We got our shirts and toothbrushes from the wagon. Harvey carried a small suitcase with his extra clothes as we walked down the street to the hotel. None of us boys had ever slept in a hotel, so it was pretty exciting. Harvey arranged for two rooms – one for him, and the other for the three of us. "They have big double size beds. Young Willie doesn't take up much room, so I think you guys can share."

"Like a bug in a rug," Willie said.

Harvey roared with laughter. "Like a bug in a rug," he repeated. "Willie, you're a gem."

We went to our rooms to wash up. Willie jumped on the bed. "Wow! It's soft as a cloud," he said as he bounced up and down.

There was a pitcher of water and a washbasin in the room, but just down the hall there were two rooms with bathtubs in them.

"I think I'll take a bath," Tone said. He took the soap and a towel from the rack and headed down the hall. Harvey was already in one of the bathrooms. A while later Tone came back wrapped in a towel, all clean looking and smelling good from the soap. I took my turn, and when Harvey was finished, Willie took a bath, too.

Willie's hair was still wet and he had soap in his left ear as he dressed in his ever-present bibs and a shirt – something new and different for him. "You missed some Willie," I said, pointing to the soap in his ear.

He looked in the mirror and wiped out the soap. "A little

different than bathing in the river, isn't it?"

"Yeah, and the water's warmer, too," I said.

Harvey knocked on our door. "You guys ready for supper?"

"Be right there, Harvey. Willie is just getting dressed."

In clean shirts and shorts, we met Harvey in the hall. He had shaved and bathed, and he wore a nice suit. "Wow, Harvey! You look like a millionaire," Willie said.

Harvey winked. "You never know."

In the dining room the waitress gave us menus. As we looked them over, Harvey said, "Get what ever you want boys, and don't worry about the price."

Tone and I ordered steak. Harvey and Willie had chicken. We talked about our adventures during the summer, so far, and the food tasted wonderful after our steady diet of fish, potatoes, and canned beef. When our plates were cleaned off, Willie leaned back, patted his stomach and uttered his famous little after dinner speech. "Whew. Stick a fork in me. I'm done!"

Harvey laughed uproariously and nearly choked. "Young Willie, you certainly can bring a lot of fun to anything you do," he said. He ruffled Willie's hair.

After we had talked some more, Mr. Honer made the announcement that he thought it was soon time for bed. "A long day awaits us tomorrow. I'll knock on your door when I get up. We'll have breakfast and get on the road. I'd like to get to Sauk City by tomorrow."

Willie collected the scraps from our dinners and asked the waitress for something to put them in. When she asked what he was going to do with them, he said, "Ahab's probably hungry, too."

"Ahab?" The waitress seemed a little startled.

Willie explained who Ahab was, and then quite dramatically told of how he had made the daring rescue in a treacherous flood to save the dog, clinging to a log for dear life. She must have been a dog lover, and maybe just a little impressed with Willie's story, because she came back with a metal bowl filled with beef and

154

mashed potatoes, and a small pail of water. "He'll like this better than those scraps," she said, smiling at Willie.

I think Willie could charm almost anyone.

Ahab was glad to see us, and was quite grateful for his supper. Willie untied him and we walked back to the hotel. I took the pan and pail back to the kitchen and thanked the waitress. Willie and Tone snuck Ahab up the back stairs to our room.

We stopped at Harvey's door, said "goodnight" and went to our room. We were all pretty tired after the long day. We took off our shirts and shorts and jumped into bed. Ahab curled up next to Willie's feet. When I turned off the lamp, in the moonlight shining through the window, I could see the corners of Willie's mouth turned up in the most contented smile.

Chapter 43

Six days, six hotels, six steak dinners, and six big comfy beds later we pulled into Wausau. It was much larger than any other city we had passed through on our journey, and it was the biggest city any of the three of us had ever seen.

"Holy smokes, Harvey," Willie exclaimed as we drove down the street. "How many people live in this town?"

"I believe about twelve thousand now," Harvey replied.

"Twelve thousand? Wow! That's a lot of people in one place," I said, gawking at all the big downtown buildings and the people walking everywhere.

And something else that we had seen little of at home – motorcars were everywhere. "Just look at them all," Tone said, pointing to a row parked along the street.

Harvey laughed. "They've been here now for a few years, and getting to be more of them all the time. Boys? The day will come when horses will be a thing of the past."

"That's hard to believe, Harvey," I said.

"They're already building motorcars that are bigger, like wagons for hauling stuff, and one of these days I'll have one, and my horses will get their retirement. Just wait and see."

We pulled up in front of a factory. A big sign on the side said: HONER CASKET COMPANY.

"Is this your company, Harvey?" Willie asked.

"Yes, young Willie, this is it. How about a tour?"

"That would be great," we all said, and jumped off the wagon to go inside with Harvey. Willie leashed Ahab with a short piece of rope so he wouldn't get into trouble.

The workers were all happy to see Harvey, greeting him and shaking his hand. He introduced us to all of them as we strolled through the factory, and when we had seen just about the whole place, a whistle blew and everyone quit working. They each picked up their lunch pails and ambled outside to picnic tables along the side of the building to eat.

156

We were still gazing at all the caskets stacked up and ready for delivery when Harvey suggested that we go down the street to a restaurant for some lunch. As we walked out the front door, several of Harvey's workers were gathered around our boat.

"What do you think of that workmanship?" Harvey asked as we approached them.

"Somebody knows wood," one man said.

"And somebody knows finish," another remarked.

Harvey pointed to Tone, Willie and me. "These lads did all the finish work on that boat. Excellent job, isn't it?"

"I did the carving on the side," Willie said proudly.

"*Voyageur.* What's that about?" one of the men asked.

"That's what they called the French explorers – the Voyageurs," I explained.

"These boys are going re-trace their journey down the river," Harvey said proudly.

The men all nodded their approval. One said, "You better hire them when they get back, Harvey. We could use someone with skill like that."

"These two bigger ones have another year of school. I wouldn't want to see them miss their education. And this little guy," Harvey said, ruffling Willie's hair, "has many years of school yet. But if they want jobs after that, I'd hire them in a minute."

Walking down the street toward the restaurant, Tone turned to Harvey. "Were you serious? I mean about hiring us?"

"As serious as I can be," Harvey said. "You ever need a job, you've always got one here."

After a nice lunch, Harvey invited us to his home for the night. "It's getting too late in the day to start out on the river. You can get a good night's sleep at my house, and I'll haul you down to the river, and your adventure can begin tomorrow." He stopped his team in front of a huge mansion.

"Is this where you live?" Willie asked incredulously.

"This is it," Harvey answered.

"You live alone in this big house?" I asked.

"I have a housekeeper and a cook. And yes, sadly, just me."

It was the grandest house I had ever seen. All the furniture looked very expensive. Carpets covered all the floors, paintings hung on the walls, and a grand piano graced the huge living room where one wall of nearly all windows overlooked the city. The next room was the library. Its walls were lined with shelves filled with books. On the other side of the main entrance hall, the kitchen was just beyond a large dining room with a fabulous chandelier hanging over a huge mahogany table.

We followed Harvey up the grand staircase to the second floor – four bedrooms and two bathrooms. All during the grand tour, Willie held Harvey's hand as if he were afraid he'd be lost. I nudged Tone and he grinned as he saw Willie with Harvey. "They're good for each other," he whispered. "One needs a son. The other needs a dad."

"Do you boys each want your own room? I have three extra rooms you know."

I stared questioningly at Tone and Willie.

"I'd just as soon share a room," Tone said. "Ladd and I have stayed at each other's houses since we were babies. It's just natural for me to share a room with him."

"And Willie, I'd be happy if you took my son's room. It's got a lot of stuff in it for a boy your age. I'm sure he'd be happy to have you enjoy it."

"Are you sure it's all right?" Willie asked.

"Yes, Willie, I'd like you sleep in his room."

"Well, okay. I guess that would be great," Willie said.

Harvey opened the door into the first bedroom. "Tone and Ladd, you can use this room. I'll show Willie to his room. Have a little rest, get cleaned up, and we'll call you for supper."

Harvey walked down the hall with Willie holding his hand. Tone smiled. "Willie's made a good friend."

Chapter 44

Tone and I took turns in the nearest upstairs bathroom. It was a grand bathroom with a big copper bathtub with hot and cold running water. After a refreshing bath, I wrapped up in one of the big thick towels and went back to the room. Tone took his turn in the bathroom while I dressed in my shorts and shirt and went to the library. Harvey had hundreds of books, everything from political essays to history. There were many on travel, and he had almost all of the classics. I was paging through a copy of *The Count of Monte Cristo* when Harvey noticed me there and came in.

"Willie tells me that you've read many books to him."

"I read almost every evening at the cabin. Willie and Tone both can read real well, but they like the way I read, so I read, and they listen."

"Nothing is more important that being able to read. No matter what you do in life, if you can read you can learn anything you need to know to succeed. I'm glad you're exposing Willie to the classics. They're *classics* for good reason – they're masterpieces."

"Yeah, that's right. And we really enjoy the stories. Did we tell you that Willie's dog got his name from *Moby Dick.*"

"Yes, you did mention that. He must be pretty fond of Ahab. I heard him talking to him in his room as I walked by," Harvey said.

"Yeah, he talks to him all the time," I laughed. "But you know the funny part? I think Ahab understands what he's talking about."

Harvey burst out laughing. "He's a fine boy. So much like my son. I've become quite fond of him."

I put the book back on the shelf.

"Take it with you, so you'll have something to read while you're camped at night," Harvey said.

"Oh, I can't do that. What if something happens to it?"

"If something happens to it, I'll replace it. If not, you can return it to me the next time I deliver caskets. Now, would you go upstairs and tell the other boys that supper is about ready."

"Okay. And thanks for the book. I'll take good care of it," I assured as I climbed the stairs.

Tone had fallen asleep. I gently shook him awake. "Wake up. Harvey says supper is ready." Then I headed down the hall for Willie's room.

I knocked and opened the door, expecting to find Willie asleep, too. But instead, he sat at the small desk looking out the window. Ahab was lying at his feet snoozing, but he woke up when I opened the door.

Willie motioned to me. "Come here and look at this." He held a notebook. The handwriting on its pages was that of a child. "This is Harvey's son's book," Willie said. "He wrote an essay about what he wanted to be when he grew up."

I looked at the notebook and began reading:

"I want to be just like my papa when I grow up. Papa is a good man who makes caskets for people to get buried in when they die. Someday I want to have a business like Papa's. All the people like him because he is such a good man. I want to help him work so he can retire and go fishing.........."

I read the rest of the essay while Willie looked on. "Do you suppose Harvey ever read that?" Willie asked.

"I don't know, Willie," I said. "But I'm sure he would be proud that his boy wanted to be like him."

"Harvey's a good man. I wish he was *my* dad," Willie said.

I hugged Willie's shoulder. "I bet he thinks the same way, Willie. C'mon. Lets go eat. I'm hungry."

We went down to the dining room. Tone and Harvey were already sitting at the table waiting for us. I felt a little out of place in the luxurious room with its fine furniture, china dishes, and linen tablecloth and napkins. Cut off jeans and bare feet just didn't seem quite right in such a fancy place.

"What's wrong Ladd?" Harvey asked. "You look uncomfortable."

"I just thought it was kind of wrong for us to be dressed in shorts and barefoot in such an elegant dining room."

Harvey laughed loudly, "It's just wood and cloth, Ladd. You boys don't need fancy clothes and shoes to show your class. You are all fine gentlemen."

Just then the housekeeper carried in a big pot of beef stew and set it on the table. She left and returned several more times with a tray with hot buns, corn on the cob, salad greens, and a big bowl of beans that she set right in front of Willie. She smiled at him as she set the dish down. "Mr. Harvey says you like beans, Master Willie, so these are just for you."

Willie grinned from ear to ear. Tone and I groaned. "Well, at least we're not going to be in the same room tonight," Tone said. Harvey roared with laughter.

After the wonderful dinner, Harvey sipped from a glass of wine and we had lemonade. "That was a great dinner, Harvey. Thank you so much," I said.

Willie slid his chair back and rubbed his belly. "Stick a fork in me..."

"You're done!" Harvey bellowed and laughed till he began choking.

We talked about the next day and how long it would take us to get back home. Harvey told us about some of the exciting things we'd see and the interesting towns we'd pass on our journey downriver. He made the trip sound even more enjoyable than we had imagined it would be.

And as the evening wore on, Willie mentioned the essay he had found, written by Harvey's son. "Have you read it, Harvey?" he asked.

Harvey smiled sadly. "Yes, Willie, I have. He wrote that just a few days before he died."

"If you don't mind telling us, how did it happen?" Tone asked.

"No I don't mind," Harvey said, and then he began. "It was

161

just a terrible accident. We were on a trip up north, to Green Bay, and I had taken David with me. He had just turned thirteen. His mama had died a few years earlier and he hated staying home alone with the housekeeper, so I often took him along in the summer time, or when he could get out of school.

"We were staying in a hotel in Green Bay and I had to meet a client after supper. The man had a funeral to attend to that day and couldn't see me until later, so I went to his funeral home for the meeting to take his order for some caskets. David wanted to stay in the room. He loved reading and was engrossed in a new book, so I left him there.

"An hour later I was at the funeral home talking to my client when we heard a fire bell ringing, but we didn't pay much attention to it. After our meeting I started back toward the hotel and when I got closer, I realized that the fire was in *our* hotel. I ran as fast as I could, but it was too late. The fire brigade had tried to get everyone out, but they were too late for David. They carried his body out of the room, but he was already dead. He had been reading the book and fell asleep on the bed. That's where they found him."

Tears rolled from Willie's eyes. "Was he burned real bad?"

"No, Willie, he wasn't burned at all. He died from the smoke. He just looked like he was sleeping."

With tears streaming down his cheeks, Willie got up from his chair and put his arms around Harvey's neck in a caressing, loving hug. "I'm real sorry, Harvey."

Harvey returned the hug. "Thanks, Willie."

We all sat in silence for a couple of minutes thinking about the loss that Harvey felt.

"Just remember one thing, boys," Harvey began again. "If you're ever caught in a fire, stay low. Get on the floor and crawl. The smoke and poison gas will go up, and the clean air is down near the floor. Always remember that. If David had known that, he might still be alive right now."

Harvey's advice instilled in us a valuable, lasting impression.

162

Chapter 45

August 4, 1914

Afaint knock on our bedroom door awoke Tone and me. Harvey's housekeeper informed us that breakfast was ready. We heard her go next door to wake Willie, too. A minute later, Willie bounded into our room. "Well, today's the day." He bubbled with eagerness.

"Yeah, Willie. Today our adventure starts. You all packed and ready?"

"I'm wearing everything I have, so I guess I'm ready. I'll take Ahab outside, and then I'll meet you guys in the dining room."

Ahab was jumping up and down, anxious to get outside, so off they went. Tone and I went downstairs and found Harvey at the table reading the newspaper. "Morning, Harvey," we both said.

Harvey looked up from the paper with a concerned expression, but then smiled broadly. "Good morning, lads. And where is young Willie?"

"Ahab had to go out. They'll be here soon," I said as I sat down.

"You look concerned about something, Harvey," Tone said. "Anything wrong?"

"I'm afraid war has broken out in Europe. Germany has declared war on Russia and now they've invaded Belgium. It won't be long and England will declare war against Germany, and who knows how long it will be before we're dragged into it?"

"Do you really think we'll get involved?" I asked.

"I'm sure we'll try to stay out of it, but I'm afraid we'll have to help before long. It's been building for a while now. I was hoping it wouldn't happen, but now it has and there's no turning back."

Willie and Ahab came running in. It seemed so natural that Willie should give Harvey a hug. "Morning, Harvey," he said with a gleaming smile.

"Good morning, young Willie. Did you sleep well?"

"Like a rock," Willie replied. "That's a great room."

"Well, then you'll have to come back and use it again sometime," Harvey said. "Well, dig in, boys. The food is getting cold."

We all piled our plates with eggs, pancakes, and bacon. There was milk and orange juice, and Tone and I each had a cup of coffee. Willie snuck some bites to Ahab under the table; Harvey pretended not to see him doing it.

"Well, I know you boys are eager to get started on your journey, so I'll haul you down to the river if you're ready," Harvey announced.

Harvey's housekeeper came through the kitchen door and handed Tone a picnic basket filled with sandwiches, fruit, cakes and cookies. We thanked her for everything.

"You come back and visit again," she said. "It was so nice to have someone here in this big, empty house." She gave Willie a big hug and patted Ahab on the head. "And you can come, too, Ahab. You're such a good boy."

The horses were all hitched up to the wagon. We all climbed aboard and Harvey headed down the street toward the river.

"Now, boys, I want you to remember... don't get careless," Harvey began. Coming from anyone else, it might have sounded like a lecture, but coming from Harvey, it was sound advice. "The river is quite different here than what you're used to. The channel is narrower and deeper, and the current is swift. And you'll have to watch ahead for the dams."

"Dams?"

"Don't get too close to them or you might get caught in the current and be swept over. Be ready to pull in to shore to portage around them. They all have trails, so you can easily carry your boat and gear to the other side."

"Dams. Cripes! I never thought of that," I said. "How many are there?"

"I've drawn you a crude map. There are ten dams between here and your part of the river, and two more are being built right now. You may be able to pass through those two yet. But with the rest of them, you'll have to watch ahead and get out on the portage trail before you get too close."

"We'll watch, Harvey," Willie said. "I don't think we want to go over the dam. It sounds exciting, but I think we'll not try it."

Harvey laughed. "Young Willie, whatever am I going to do without your wit?"

We drove to the river just below the new Wausau dam, which was still under construction. "The old dam is upriver a few miles," Harvey said. "This one will be finished next year." He pointed to the map he'd given us. "The next dam is about ten miles downriver at Rothschild, so keep an eye out."

We slid Voyageur off the wagon, carried it to the riverbank, and loaded our gear into it.

"Well, Harvey," I said. "We can't thank you enough for everything you've done for us. We'll never forget you for it." Tone and I shook hands with Harvey and he gave us each a good-bye hug.

"You're the best, Harvey," Willie said as he hugged Harvey's chest. Harvey put his arms around Willie and said, "You have a wonderful trip, and I'll see you soon."

"Are you coming back to deliver more caskets soon?" Willie asked.

"You never know when I might show up, Willie. I might come just to visit."

Willie climbed into the boat and sat at the middle on the rolled up tarp. "C'mon, Ahab. Let's go!" he called to the dog. Ahab scampered over from some bushes and jumped into the boat. Tone and I pushed off and began paddling out into the current. Harvey stood on the bank and waved as we slid downstream and rounded the first bend.

Willie turned and waved just as Harvey disappeared from sight.

"You and Harvey are pretty good friends," I said.

Willie nodded and wiped a tear from his cheek.

Chapter 46

ere in the north, the river is much narrower than it is at home. We were used to a wide, shallow river with sandbars and islands dotting the surface, and our river bluffs were a mile away on each side of the channel. Here the bluffs were often right at the edge of the river with towering cliffs and sheer rock faces bordering the dark, tea colored water. I had read somewhere that the dark color was caused by tannic acid in the Tamarack swamps emptying into the northern river.

The fast current carried *Voyageur* along with very little paddling, except to keep it heading straight. It was a beautiful day and we just took our time floating along, watching the scenery slip by. Time passed quickly and sooner than we expected, as we came around a bend we could see the Rothschild dam ahead.

"Let's paddle over to the side so we can find the portage trail," I said to Tone. I wasn't up to taking any unnecessary chances this early in the trip.

We navigated Voyageur near the bank where we noticed a sign on the shore that said:

BEWARE!

DAM AHEAD

PORTAGE TRAIL AHEAD 100 YARDS

We found a little gravel landing and pulled the boat up on the shore. Instead of a sandy beach like we were used to, the bank was all gravel and stones, washed and smoothed with rounded edges from centuries of rubbing together in the river current. Ahab bounded out of the boat and raised his leg on the nearest tree. Willie mimicked the dog. He lifted one leg and peed on the tree, too.

Tone and I began laughing so hard we could hardly sit up. "Willie, you nut. Sometimes I wonder about you."

Willie looked over his shoulder, lowered his leg and scratched in the gravel with his foot, grinning like a lunatic.

We unloaded the boat and Tone and I lifted it up on our shoulders, following the trail over the hill to the lower side of the dam. The path was gravel and not too steep, so it was easy to get across the dam. Willie carried the picnic basket, and while he and Ahab guarded the boat, Tone and I went back to get the rest of the gear.

When everything was reloaded again, we slid off down the river, and in about three hours we portaged around the Mosinee dam. Downriver a few more miles we pulled up on a gravel bar, had some lunch, went for a swim, and then decided to have a little nap. We used our blankets there because the gravel wasn't as nice and soft as the sand we were used to.

Tone woke me a couple of hours later, tickling my nose with a weed. I sleepily batted at what I thought was an insect several times, and then I heard Tone and Willie giggling. I opened my eyes and there they were, kneeling over me. "Wise guys!" I said and grabbed Tone, wrestling him to the ground. We rolled over and over and Ahab ran around us, barking his head off thinking it was a wonderful game. Seconds later Willie jumped on top of us and we all rolled into the river. Ahab wanted to join the fun, too. He launched himself off the gravel bar and splashed down right in the middle of the pack.

We goofed around in the water for a while until we decided to move on downriver to find a good spot to camp for the night.

We found a nice island with a lot of dry driftwood piled on its banks, probably by floodwaters that spring. We turned the boat on its side and built our shelter as we had practiced. After supper we all sat around the campfire and I finished reading *Huckleberry Finn:*

"If I'd a knowed what trouble it was to make a book I wouldn't a tackled it, and ain't a goin to no more. But I reckon I got to light out for the Territory ahead of the rest, because Aunt Sally she's going to adopt me and sivilize me, and I can't stand it. I been there before."

"Gosh, that was good," Willie said as I closed the book. "Do you suppose our adventure will be as exciting as Huck's?"

"I doubt that we'll meet up with such characters as Huck did, Willie, but you never know."

Chapter 47

For the next two days we paddled, swam, fished and enjoyed our journey down the river. We saw pines and birch and tamarack here, unlike lots of oaks and maples that we were used to seeing along the river bluffs at home. Eagles soared over the bluffs riding the thermals that rose up and carried them for hours without ever flapping a wing.

We portaged the Jackson Mill dam early in the morning of the second day and then paddled past the city of Stevens Point. We thought about stopping for groceries, but our picnic hamper still had plenty of food yet, so we just went on. Later in the day we portaged the Upper Paper Mill dam and then camped for the night a few miles below it on a nice island. I began reading *The Count of Monte Cristo* by the light of the campfire.

Day three we paddled the next ten miles to the Whiting/Plover dam and portaged. We were getting pretty good at it, and could get all of our gear around most of the dams in less than an hour. When we got to the Biron dam, construction equipment lined the portage trail. Part of the dam had failed the previous year and the re-building was in progress. The men working on the dam had to stop and visit with us, and took special interest in Willie and Ahab. Willie had taught Ahab some tricks: sit, beg, roll over, and dead dog, and the men enjoyed the show immensely.

By the time we reached Wisconsin Rapids, we needed some groceries and decided to take a look at the town. We hid *Voyageur* in the brush and walked the road into the city. Ahab came to town with us, and much to his dismay, tied to a short piece of rope. He much preferred his freedom, but we couldn't take a chance that he might get into trouble, or lost, so he had to be leashed. We found a general store and bought our supplies – eggs and bacon and some sausages to roast over the fire, and we even splurged for some penny candy for Willie.

Eight miles below Wisconsin Rapids at Centralia, part of the river was blocked with the construction of a new dam, but the other half was open so we just paddled through. All the current funneled through that open part of the river and we slipped through like riding down wild rapids.

We camped just above Port Edwards that night. As we were sitting by the fire, Willie studied the map Harvey had drawn for us showing the dams and the approximate distance between them. "Looks like we've only got four more dams to go around," he said. "Then it's open river all the way home."

"Are you getting homesick?" I asked.

"No! Jeez, no. I kinda miss Ma, but not my sisters. I miss the cabin more than anything."

"The cabin will be there when we get back," Tone said. "It's built real sturdy, and it should last quite a few years... unless we get a really big flood."

"Maybe next year we can live there again," Willie said.

"We'll probably have to get jobs next summer, or maybe by then Tone and I will have to be soldiers in the war."

"I hope that doesn't happen."

"Well, if it does, maybe you and Ronnie can spend the summer on the island," Tone suggested.

"Yeah, that might be okay, and we'll have Ahab for a guard dog."

Ahab heard his name and looked up.

"You a guard dog, Ahab?"

Ahab laid his chin back on his paws and went back to sleep.

"I guess not," Willie said.

The next day we passed Port Edwards and then Nekoosa. Our map showed open river for a long way. There weren't many towns or roads, and the country looked wild and primitive.

"This is what it was like when Father Marquette came past here," I said.

We camped on an island that night, and paddled all the next day without having to portage. Occasionally, we'd pass a log house built near the river, some with a barn nearby and a few cows grazing along the grassy bank. At one of the little farms, two boys were fishing from a wooden dock in front of the house. They waved to us and lifted a stringer of fish, showing us their catch.

The river flowed fast and deep and we floated along at a good pace, and because there had not been any dams to slow us down, we estimated that we had covered nearly fifty miles that day.

On day seven we portaged the Kilbourn dam, and stopped for the night just above another new dam construction site at Prairie du Sac. We wouldn't have to portage that one; we could just paddle right by it the next morning.

"Well, tomorrow we'll be starting the last fifty miles of river," Tone said.

"Maybe one more stop about half way, and we should be home the next day," I said, looking to the western horizon.

But plans are always subject to change.

Chapter 48

August 12, 1914

We got an early start after a big breakfast and paddled through the open end of the new dam at Prairie du Sac. From there, the river was open the rest of the way to the Mississippi, if we wanted to go that far. Of course, we'd be stopping at home, instead.

The river was getting shallower and much wider. Now we were seeing many of the more familiar sandbars, and we had to be more careful where we paddled, or we'd find ourselves stuck on one of them. That would only interrupt a pleasant day.

We found a nice, dry sandbar where we ate our lunch and had a good nap. But when we woke up in mid-afternoon, we could hear thunder far off in the distance.

"It's gonna storm," Willie said, looking to the west. Wind gusts whipped around us now and then, and big, black thunderclouds were building up and looked pretty threatening.

"Let's try to get to Spring Green," I said. "We can find a place to camp there, and maybe get some groceries."

"I just hope we can get there before that storm hits," Tone said.

We paddled hard for about an hour and a half and we were just passing under the Spring Green bridge when a strong, gusty wind came right up the river into our faces. We struggled to keep the front of the boat headed downriver, as the gusts turned us to the side every time they hit us.

"Head over toward the bank," I yelled, trying to make myself heard above the wind noise. "We're gonna have to find a place to take shelter if this storm hits."

As we headed toward the bank, Willie pointed and said, "Hey, look! There's a man on that dock over there. Maybe he can show us a place to get in from the storm."

Sure enough, there was a man standing on a strange-looking

dock that appeared to be nothing more than a slab of concrete sticking out of the river bank about three feet above the water. He was dressed in a suit and wore a wide brimmed hat with a flat top.

He stood with his back to us, gazing at the storm clouds that were getting closer and closer. Just as we came even with him on the river, a gust of wind blew his hat off his head. He grabbed for it, but it sailed out over the river and came down just beyond our boat. Willie saw the hat floating. He stood up, unhooked the straps on his bib shorts, let them drop to his feet, and dove over the side of the boat into the river, all in one graceful motion. Ahab was about half a second behind him.

Willie came to the surface and swam toward the swiftly moving hat. He caught it just as it was about to sink out of site, put it on his head and turned to swim back to the boat. By then he was quite a ways downriver and closer to the shore than he was to the boat, so I shouted to him, "Willie, just swim to the bank. We'll come and get you."

Ahab was right with him as he swam to the riverbank. They came up on the sandy shore several yards below the man and the dock. With Ahab on his heels, he ran up the bank, climbed onto the dock, and as he handed the somewhat soggy hat to the seemingly amazed man he said, "Here's your hat, mister."

"Why, thank you, young man. That was quite a show," the man said.

"I've spent most of the summer in the river, and it was fun to see if I could catch your hat." Willie beamed a wide smile.

"Well, I'm very glad to get it back. It's kind of my trademark. People recognize me because I always wear this hat when I work."

By then, Tone and I had beached the boat below the dock and had walked up to where Willie and the man were talking.

"These are my friends, Tone and Ladd," Willie informed the man. "We've spent the summer on the river together."

"Hello, sir," we both said.

"Hello, gentlemen. Nice to meet you." He offered his hand as he stared at *Voyageur.* "Where did you get that exquisite boat?"

"Tone's dad designed it, and he and my dad built it," I said.

"It's wonderful. Such elegant lines. Such a sleek look. I've never seen a finer watercraft. Very well engineered, and they did a magnificent job on the finish, too," he said.

"Ladd and Willie and I did the finish," Tone said.

"Well, you boys do very nice work. What kind of wood is that?"

We laughed. "Would you believe it's pine from packing crates that caskets were shipped in?" I said.

He seemed a bit startled... and amazed. "I'd never have guessed that. It truly is wonderful. You should be very proud of it."

"We are, sir," Tone said.

A violent bolt of lightning struck somewhere downriver. "It's going to be a bad storm," the man said. "Look at those clouds. They're just boiling. I wouldn't be surprised if a tornado came out of this one."

"We'd better find someplace to get our shelter up real soon," Willie said. "It's gonna be a cold rainy night, I'm afraid."

"Do you plan on making a tent in this wind?"

"We use the boat and a tarp, but we've never tried it in wind like this."

"I've got plenty of room in my home. Tie your boat down and come share my humble house with me and my companions?"

Another bolt of lightning flashed and thunder boomed. We decided to take advantage of his generous offer.

"That would be great, Mr...."

"Wright. Frank Lloyd Wright."

Chapter 49

We found our clothes and toothbrushes, lifted the boat onto the dock, carefully tipped it upside down, and placed it over the top of the rest of our gear.

"Tie that rope over one end, then take it under the dock and cinch the other end down. That should keep it from blowing away," Mr. Wright said.

Willie scampered under the dock with one end of the rope as I tied my end to the boat. Tone took the rope from Willie and secured the other end of the boat. When it was firmly anchored to the dock, Willie climbed out from under the big slab. "Hey, what's holding this dock up?" he asked curiously.

Mr. Wright smiled. "That's what we call a cantilever, Willie. The dock is anchored back under the embankment and it sits on a pier of cement. This slab is reinforced so it will bear the weight of itself and still hang out over the river without support."

"You know a lot about that stuff?" Willie asked.

"I'm an architect. That's my job to know about that *stuff*," Mr. Wright replied.

Lightning flashed, abruptly accompanied by a deafening clap of thunder. "That one was pretty close. We'd better head up to the house, boys. We can talk there"

"What about Ahab? Is it okay if he comes too?" Willie asked expectantly.

"Of course, Ahab is welcome, too," Mr. Wright answered. "He doesn't like being out in a storm any more than you do."

We followed Mr. Wright up the path through the trees. Suddenly the woods opened up, and there on a knoll sat the most unusual house I had ever seen. Built of stone and timbers, it looked like many different pieces of a puzzle that rose and fell and stuck out at strange angles. To get to the house, a bridge crossed a large pond and a courtyard below.

"That's your house?" I asked incredulously?

"Yes, that's my home – Taliesin."

"Taliesin? You named your home?"

Mr. Wright laughed. "Yes, I guess I'm a bit of an eccentric. The word Taliesin means *shining brow* in the Welsh language. See how it sits on the brow of the hill? I thought that was an appropriate name for it."

"It's a wonderful house," Tone said, as he took in some of the strange architecture.

"Holy smokes, Mr. Wright. You must be rich," Willie said.

Mr. Wright laughed again. "I've done pretty well in the architecture business, Willie."

"Sorry if we're so uninformed, sir, but are you famous?" Tone asked.

"Well, I'm pretty well known, world wide. But I suppose in small town Wisconsin, maybe not so much."

"World wide?" I said. "Have you built things all over the world?

"I just finished the Imperial Hotel in Japan a while back," Wright said. "And I've built homes and commercial buildings all over the country. Come, let me show you around."

We entered through the front door. I had never seen anything quite like this before. It was elegant and wonderful looking. Nothing about it was like other homes. The walls were of stone and wood with some of the furniture built right into them. The rooms seemed to flow from one to the other. Ahab was fascinated too, running across the stone floors, sniffing at everything, taking in all the wonderful new scents.

Mr. Wright led us into a room that stuck out over the side of the hill, many feet above the ground.

"This is cantilevered." Willie smiled brilliantly.

"Right you are, Willie. Bravo!"

Outside, the storm raged. Trees were whipping back and forth and the wind scattered dust and leaves. There came a tremendous clap of thunder and then the rain began coming down in sheets. Peering out of the huge windows that overlooked the valley, I could see we were right in the middle of the storm, and glad that we were inside, safe and sound.

"We came inside just in time," Mr. Wright said. "Come, I'll show you to the bunk house and then we'll see if the cook can scare up some food for you."

We followed Mr. Wright through the house past some new looking rooms that weren't quite finished. "We've added a studio and I'll be having some apprentices working here as soon as we finish things up. That's why we have this bunk house, so they can stay here while they study."

He opened a door and motioned us into the room. Inside were several men, some reading and others playing cards. "Gentlemen, I'd like you to welcome these young lads for the evening. I've offered them shelter from the storm. Please show them where they can sleep, and direct them to the kitchen once they're settled in. I'll have Mrs. Carlton fix them something to eat since they missed our supper."

One of the younger men rose and said, "Follow me, guys." We walked to the other end of the room where he pointed out two beds. "There's one double bed no one's using, and one top bunk."

"I'll take the bunk bed," Willie said. He climbed up the ladder and gave the bed a test.

"This will be great," I said. "Lots better than sleeping under a boat on the sand in the middle of a storm."

I offered my hand. "I'm Ladd, and this is my friend Tone, and that's Willie," I said, nodding to the rascal grinning at us.

"I'm Ernest Weston," the young man said. "Just call me Ernie. I work here with my father. He's the big guy over there in the blue shirt. He's the foreman." Ernest was about the same age as Tone and me, smaller, but looked to be quite strong. His dark hair and brown eyes cast a wide, friendly smile.

"Nice to meet you, Ernie," Willie said.

"Same here, Willie," he replied. "Come on. I'll show you the kitchen."

We were hungry so he didn't have to tell us twice to follow.

Chapter 50

W e followed Ernie through the house to the kitchen. As we walked in, a black lady was putting plates and silverware on a small table against the wall.

"Hello, boys," she said with a smile. "Mr. Wright said I had some hungry boys to feed. Ernie? Are you going to eat again?"

Ernie grinned. "Maybe just another piece of pie, Gertie." He turned to us again. "Guys, this is Mrs. Carlton – Gertrude – but we call her Gertie. Gertie, this is Ladd, Tone, and the little guy is Willie."

"Hello, Gertie," Tone and I greeted the cook.

"How nice to meet you all. And who is this little furry one?"

"Pleased to meet you, ma'am," Willie said. "This is my dog, Ahab. He's hungry, too."

"My, aren't you boys tan! You must have been in the sun all summer. Here. Sit, sit. Have something to eat. I know boys; they're always hungry." On the table were dishes of roast beef, mashed potatoes and green beans, and a fresh loaf of bread perched on a little cutting board. Gertie handed Willie an empty pie pan and said he should fill it with food for Ahab. Then she got a bigger pan and filled it with water for him. "You take that pan with you to the bunk house, so he can have a drink when he gets thirsty." She reached down and scratched Ahab behind the ears and he licked her hand profusely.

Ernie joined us at the table while we filled our plates with delicious food. He just had a cup of coffee. "So what are you guys doing on the river?" he asked.

We told him about our cabin and our trip from Wausau and our idea to follow the route of the Voyageurs.

"We didn't think about all the dams that have been built since then though," Willie moaned. "I think we walked almost as much as we paddled doing all those portages."

"So you've spent the whole summer on the river? What fun! I've been *working* all summer. I'm finished with school, so Pa got me this job. But I like it here, though. Mr. Wright is real good to me."

"He seems very nice," I said. "How old are you, Ernie?"

"I just turned eighteen. How about you?"

"Ladd and I are sixteen, and Willie is twelve."

"And a half," Willie piped up.

"And a half," Tone grinned.

We ate our fill and then Ernie had some apple pie with us. We thanked Gertie for the delicious food and Ernie led us back to the bunkhouse. He introduced us to the rest of the men there.

"This is my father, William. He's the boss around here, and this is Herman Fritz, from Chicago." We shook hands with the two men and introduced ourselves. "This is Emil Brodelle," Ernie continued. "He's an architectural draftsman and an apprentice to Mr. Wright." Mr. Brodelle, a young man, greeted us with a big smile and strong handshake.

"And this is Thomas Brunker. He works with the horses and animals." Mr. Brunker greeted us. "I run the farm and take care of the outbuildings."

"And last but not least, is David Lindblom, who is our gardener." Ernie nodded toward a young man with blonde hair and a big smile.

I noticed an accent as Lindblom greeted us. "Where are you from, Mr. Lindblom?" I asked.

"Please call me David, and I come from Sweden," he said.

"Ah," I said. "My grandparents are from Norway. You sound a little like them."

He laughed. "Ya, ve all sound alike from de old country."

We all chatted and got to know each other, and Willie and Ahab entertained the group with tall tales and dog tricks. About ten o'clock some of the older men decided to turn in, so we all took our turn in the bathroom and soon we were all bunked down. Willie was just across the room from us in the top bunk over Ernie. Ahab was lying on the floor below the bed, and after everyone had quit stirring, he quietly jumped up on the bed and curled up near Ernie's feet. The movement woke up Ernie. He saw Ahab there and then whispered to the dog. Ahab's tail wagged and he crawled up next to Ernie's chest and snuggled down. Ernie grinned at me. "I like dogs," he said as he snuggled with Ahab. Ahab loved the attention and gave Ernie a big wet lick on his face.

I poked Tone and motioned toward the dog. Tone grinned. "Willie's got him spoiled."

Chapter 51

August 13

"Where did you come from?" a small voice said. I was still half asleep and it took me a second or two to figure out that the voice was coming from beside the bed. I opened my eyes to see a small boy standing there staring at me.

He was a little shorter than Willie but probably about the same age. He had thick curly brown hair, inquisitive brown eyes and was dressed in a pair of red shorts and a blue and white striped tee shirt. "Good morning," he said. "Where did you come from?"

"We were paddling down the river late yesterday afternoon," I said. "Mr. Wright met us and offered to let us sleep here... so we could get out of the storm."

He nodded as if he understood. Just then Ahab jumped off of Ernie's bed, trotted over to the boy and licked the back of his leg. The boy jumped when he felt the wet tongue on his leg, turned and saw Ahab there, wagging his tail. "And who are you?" he asked.

"His name is Ahab, and he's my dog," Willie said from the top bunk.

"Another one! I didn't see you up there. Are you with these boys, too?"

"Yup. Who are you?"

"My name is John Cheney. My mama is a friend of Mr. Wright's, and we live here with him. What's your name?"

"I'm Willie, and that guy next to you is Ladd, and the other one is Tone. We've been living on the river all summer in a cabin that we built ourselves."

"No fooling? That sounds like fun. How old are you?" he asked Willie.

"I'm twelve and a half. How bout you?"

"I'm eleven… and a half," he said with a smile.

Willie jumped down from the bed and walked across the room. He stuck out his hand and shook hands with John Cheney. "Nice to meet you," he said.

Tone and I got up, pulled on our shorts and shirts and went to the bathroom to wash while the two little guys got to know each other. By the time we returned, Willie was in his bib overall shorts and had his shirt on, which was unusual for him. "John invited us to have breakfast with him and his family," he said.

"Are you sure it's all right?" I asked.

"I'm sure. Mr. Wright has had his breakfast. I was talking to him earlier, and he told me to come to the bunkhouse. Said I'd be surprised, so I guess you guys must be the surprise. Mama and my sister, Martha will be waiting for us, so we'd better go."

John led us through the house to what he called the "dining porch." With a whole wall of windows, the family's dining room overlooked a valley vista. The view was fabulous.

"Well here are our guests," his mother said as we entered the room.

"Mama, this is Willie, Ladd and Tone. And this is Ahab, Willie's dog."

"Well, good morning, boys. Frank had to go to town to the telegraph office. Please sit down and have some breakfast with us. This is John's sister, Martha," she said, nodding to the little girl, probably about nine years old.

"Frank told me that you rescued his favorite hat yesterday, and that you spent the night in the bunkhouse. What a frightful storm, it's a good thing you didn't have to camp out in that."

"Yes ma'am, we were lucky to meet Mr. Wright, or we'd be pretty cold and miserable right now instead of sitting at this nice breakfast table," Tone said with a charming smile."

"Please call me Mamah. That's my name. I feel old when people call me ma'am."

"Mamah – that's an unusual name. I don't think I've ever heard that before," I said.

"It's an old name that's not very common, but I'm stuck with it," she sighed. She was a very pretty lady with dark curly hair like John's and a warm smile. Little Martha had the same features, and she smiled shyly when Tone winked at her.

A large black man carried a silver tray into the room, set it on a sideboard, and began setting the dishes from it onto the table.

"Boys, this is Julian Carlton. His wife is our cook... I believe you met her last evening."

"Good morning, gentlemen," Julian said.

"Good morning, Mr. Carlton," we all said in unison.

"Your wife is a very good cook," Willie said. "She gave us a real good supper last night."

"I'm happy you liked it," he said dryly. He finished serving the breakfast and then asked Mamah, "Will there be anything else?"

"No, Julian, thank you," she replied. He turned and left the room. Mamah waited a few seconds and then said in a low voice, "Julian is a little abrupt, so don't take it as if he doesn't like you. He's just not very talkative."

We accepted the explanation and quietly began eating. After a couple of minutes of silence, Mamah said, "So tell me about your adventures this summer. I hear you've been on quite a journey."

Willie began the story and the family sat enthralled with his rendition of our experiences. Tone winked at me as Willie told the story about rescuing Ahab. The water seemed to get deeper and the current swifter every time he told it. When he came to the part about how we fooled Mr. Meyer, John shrieked with laughter.

"Ma, can they stay with us for a while?" he begged. "I haven't had anyone to play with all summer. I wanna show Willie all my good forts and stuff! Can they stay? Please?"

"I'm sure they're welcome to stay, John. But it's up to them."

Chapter 52

Willie was just finishing the part of the story about portaging around the dams when Mr. Wright walked into the room. "Well, I see everyone is up and ready for a big day."

"Good morning, Mr. Wright. Thanks to you we're all warm and full of breakfast." Tone flashed one of his dazzling smiles.

"Happy to have you as guests," Mr. Wright returned.

"Willie has been entertaining us with tales of their exploits this summer. It seems they've been living off the land on an island in the river," Mamah said. "Isn't that interesting?"

"Yes, a summer to remember," Wright remarked. Then he turned to us and said, "Boys, I have a proposition for you. If you remember the addition I showed you last evening – the drafting room for the school? If you recall, the ceiling has several natural wood beams. Would you care to work for me a couple of days to finish those beams? You did such a wonderful job on your boat, and I'd like to get that same rich finish on those beams."

I glanced at Tone and he shrugged his shoulders. "I guess we could do it. School starts next week so we have to get home, but we still have a few days. And it shouldn't take much more than a day to get home from here. Do you know how far it is to Muscoda?"

"Twenty six miles exactly. I was born in Richland Center, so I know that area very well," Mr. Wright said. "I'm sure you can paddle it in a day if there's no wind; a day and a half if it gets windy. I'll pay you a dollar each, plus all the good food you can eat while you're here."

"Sounds like a good deal to me," I said.

"Ma, can I show Willie my room and take him up on the hill and show him the place?" John asked.

"I think that will be just fine John, unless Ladd and Tone need him to help them "

"No, go ahead," I told Willie. "You guys have fun. We'll do the finishing."

"I have to go to Chicago," Mr. Wright announced. "I just got a cable and I'm needed for some consultations on a building that is under construction, so I'll have to leave. But, I'll see to it that Mr. Weston knows what you're doing, and he'll get all the materials you need."

"That will be fine with us, Mr. Wright. Thanks for your hospitality and all. It will be a pleasure to work on such a magnificent house."

Mr. Wright and Mamah left the breakfast room and Martha went to her room to play. Willie and John and Ahab hurried off to do what boys that age do, and Tone and I went to find Mr. Weston so we could start working on the beams. Mr. Carlton came in just as we were leaving. Tone asked him if we could help him clear the dishes away.

"Don't need no help," he said brusquely.

On the way back to the bunkhouse, Tone quietly said to me, "That Julian seems to be an angry man. I wonder what he's so mad about?"

"I don't know, but I think we should just keep out of his way as best we can."

Mr. Weston escorted us to a tool shed and found the varnish, brushes, and sandpaper. We took the supplies to the unfinished room, and a few minutes later, Mr. Weston brought in some ladders. We began working on the beams.

With no curves or corners, the straight beams weren't a difficult job. We had the first coat of varnish on in no time. While we waited for it to dry, we sat outside in the shade enjoying the summer breeze.

Tone poked me in the side and pointed. Willie and John were climbing in a big tree on top of the hill, while Ahab jumped up and down, barking and wanting to get up into the tree with them. Willie was in his usual summer attire – his bib shorts – and John was shirtless and barefoot, too.

"Willie's going to have John turning native in no time," Tone said.

"I'll bet he's glad to have someone his own age to play with." We watched the two playing some kind of pretend game. They each had a sharpened stick they wielded like swords and were slaying some imagined monsters or enemies of some sort. We both laid back and in a short time we dozed off. After our nap, we went back to the room to see if the varnish was dry. It was, so we sanded the first coat and applied the second. We spent the rest of the day the same way, with a break for lunch. Willie and John came running into the dining room, nearly naked, and each grabbed a handful of ham and some bread from the table, and off they went again, back to the woods. Ahab was right behind them.

"They will be some tired young boys by nightfall," Mr. Lindblom said.

Chapter 53

By dinnertime, the beams were beginning to look really good. We were waiting for the sixth coat to dry and were eating dinner with most of the men who worked for Mr. Wright. They had their own dining room.

Little John had begged his mother to let him eat there, too, with his new best friend Willie, and she had agreed, so the two little guys were entertaining us with their childish humor. They had been running and climbing all day, and by the looks of them they had either been in the river or the pond that was on the grounds. Their legs and feet were muddy and their hair was all snarled; it had been wet and just dried where it fell.

"Have you two been behaving today?" I asked.

"Who? Us?" Willie asked with a look of innocence.

We all laughed. Just as we were finishing dinner, Mamah and little Martha came into the dining room. Mamah talked to Mr. Weston about something and then peered at Willie and John sitting at the table in their shorts without shirts or shoes. "You two look like heathens."

Martha rolled her eyes and acted like the two boys had offended her terribly. "Those boys are just P-I-G pigs!" she said as she put her hands on her hips and shook her head. Mamah burst out laughing and so did the rest of us.

"You better come along now, John. Let these gentlemen have a rest from your silliness." his mother said.

"Oh, c'mon, Ma! We're having fun," John whined. "This is the first time all summer I've had anyone to play with 'cept Martha."

His mother just smiled and shook her head. "You get a good bath before bed. I won't have those filthy feet on the clean sheets."

"Yes, Ma," John said.

Willie giggled.

"You too, Mr. Willie. A bath before bed. It's required in my house."

"Yes, ma'am," Willie said sheepishly.

The rest of us had to stifle a laugh as the two little guys tried to look serious.

Mamah told John that he could stay for one hour longer, and then she and Martha said goodnight to us and left.

"We're gonna to try to finish the beams tonight, Mr. Weston," Tone said. "Just another three or four coats. And if we get it done tonight, we'll sleep late in the morning, and get back on the river tomorrow afternoon. We really should be home soon, or our parents will be worrying about us."

"That's fine, boys. I'm sure Mr. Wright will be real happy with your work. I looked at them earlier and they are looking very good."

Tone and I checked the beams. They were dry, so we sanded them, applied coat number seven, and went out on the porch to watch the sunset. People were coming and going all night, and the house finally quieted down about eleven o'clock. We had a couple more coats to apply so we kept at it until almost three o'clock in the morning when we finally finished. We put the lid on the varnish can, cleaned our brushes, and went back to the bunkhouse. We were dead tired, and after washing up we climbed into our bed. Willie was asleep on his top bunk. Ahab was stretched out on the foot end of Ernie's bed.

I turned out the light and as my eyes adjusted to the dark room I thought I saw someone look in the door. I thought it looked like Mr. Carlton, but I wasn't sure if I had seen anyone at all. I watched a few more minutes, and then sleep overtook me.

Chapter 54

August 14, 1914

6:00 AM

* We leave the boys, now, for a short time to join the activities elsewhere in the household. An important event is taking shape that Ladd, Tone, and Willie do not see in its early stages of development. We will rejoin them a little later.

Julian Carlton and Gertrude yawned and stretched as their alarm clock rang. Mrs. Carlton got up, washed, dressed, and headed to the kitchen to begin a batch of biscuits for breakfast. Julian sat on the edge of the bed, his head still groggy from a night of tossing and turning, thinking about the plan he had formulated while lying awake in the dark. Today would be the day.

He'd show these rich white folks. They'd see that they couldn't boss him around. He hated it here in the country and longed to be back in Chicago where he and his wife had lived before Mr. Wright hired them. He didn't want to leave the city, but Gertrude thought it would be nice to live in the country. And all these bossy young men who thought he was just a servant. He'd show them. He had it all planned. Today would be a day that no one would forget.

He dressed, went to the kitchen, took a ring of keys from the hook inside the spice cupboard, and walked out into the darkness. Gertrude asked him if he wanted coffee, but he didn't respond, as if he hadn't even heard her question. The rising sun was just beginning to turn the sky dark blue in the east. In a few minutes the sky would brighten, and the Day of Atonement would begin.

He began going from door to door, locking them and making sure that each was secure. He went to the new wing, where the architectural studio and three new rooms had been added – Mrs.

189

Borthwick's breakfast porch, the workers dining room, and the bunkhouse – and locked all of the outside doors. Anyone leaving the three rooms would have to go into the hallway and exit through the door that opened into the inner courtyard at the end of the hall. It was the only outside door left unlocked.

He didn't bother to lock the new classroom with the beams now all varnished and beautiful. It was on the backside of the house, and no one could get to it without first coming into the hallway of the new addition.

With all the doors locked, Julian searched through the tool shed until he found a hatchet, wrapped a rag around its head, and slipped it inside his jacket. From the barrel of gasoline used for running the tractor and generator, he filled an empty metal pail.

He hid the hatchet and gasoline behind some shrubs near the door in the courtyard, and then he went back to the kitchen and had his breakfast.

Mrs. Carlton tried to engage him in conversation, but he wasn't in the mood for talking. "What's wrong with you this morning, Julian. You act like you have something on your mind."

"Nothin' wrong. Just didn't sleep well," he said. He didn't want to talk. He had to concentrate on his plan – his plan to show them all just who they were dealing with.

Gertie was putting the breakfast for the family and the workers on trays to be taken to the dining rooms. Soon they would all see what Julian had in mind.

Chapter 55

7:00 AM

E mil Brodelle was awake lying in his bed watching the clock as it ticked closer to 7 o'clock. He got up and shut the alarm off just before it would start ringing. Quietly he shook Thomas Brunker awake, holding his finger up to his mouth as a sign to be quiet. "The boys were up finishing those beams until after three o'clock. Let's not wake them."

Brunker nodded and swung his legs out of the bed, yawning and stretching. Then he quietly woke Ernie Weston, whispering to be quiet. "Don't wake the guests... they were up working quite late. We're going to let them sleep in."

Ernie sat up on the edge of the bed and came fully awake. He stretched and nodded that he understood, petted Ahab and whispered to him to lie back down. The dog burrowed into his blankets and went back to sleep.

Brodelle awakened David Lindblom, and soon the four men were dressed and taking turns in the bathroom, getting ready for breakfast. As they finished in the bathroom, one by one they drifted down the hallway to the dining room.

William Weston had already been up for half an hour and had checked the beams in the new classroom. He was very pleased with the job the boys had done, and he intended to tell them so, right after they were up. As he walked back to the bunkhouse he noticed Julian Carlton coming from the garden shed. He waved and said "good morning" but Julian acted as if he hadn't heard the greeting and walked on. Weston knew Carlton's unsocial ways, so he thought nothing of it.

When Mr. Weston came into the hallway from the courtyard, Herman Fritz was just returning from his morning walk. Herman was a city person, and living in the country intrigued him, so he was in the habit of rising early to enjoy a brisk two or three mile walk through the countryside each morning.

"Morning, Herman. Have a nice walk?" William asked.

"Yes. A lovely morning, and it's going to be a fine day, William. But it looks like another hot one again."

In the house, Mrs. Borthwick was trying to get John awake for breakfast.

"I'm too tired for breakfast. I'm gonna sleep a while."

"And ten minutes after we're all done eating, you'll be pestering poor Mrs. Carlton for something to eat," Mamah lectured. "No, you get up and get going. I think Willie is leaving today. Don't you want to see him off?"

When he heard that, John got up. "Are they leaving already? I thought Tone and Ladd were doing some work for Mr. Wright."

"I believe they finished it last night, dear."

"Can't you find more work for them? I like Willie, and we had a lot of fun yesterday. Maybe they could do some other stuff so Willie can stay for a few more days."

Mamah smiled tenderly. "I'm sure Willie enjoyed playing with you, too, but he has to get back home. He has a family who misses him, and his school is starting soon, and you know, so will yours."

"You two act like savages, anyway," Martha scolded.

"Ma, tell her it's none of her business," John whined, and Martha stuck her tongue out.

"Come on, both of you. Get dressed and washed up for breakfast. And John, that means shoes and socks and a shirt."

"Awe, Ma!"

Reluctantly, the two little kids obeyed their mother's orders. Martha put on her favorite dark blue dress with the white lace collar, and John, his favorite pair of blue shorts and a bright yellow shirt. He hurriedly stroked a comb through his curly hair and headed for the breakfast room. He planned on eating quickly, so he could spend some time with Willie and Ahab before they left for home.

Chapter 56

7:50 AM

Julian Carlton served the breakfast to the family in the breakfast room, and to the men in their dining room. When he brought the trays back to the kitchen, he told his wife that he had some cleaning to do on a rug, and that he would help her pick up the dishes after everyone had finished eating.

Mamah and Martha discussed school that would start in just over a week, while John shoveled food into his mouth as fast as he could so he could be with his friend, Willie, as soon as possible.

In the employees' dining room, the men discussed the work that Mr. Weston had scheduled for the day. Ernie was just finishing his breakfast when a questioning look occupied his face. He sniffed the air, turned to his father and said, "Dad, do you smell gasoline?"

His father sniffed the air. "Yes, I do. That's odd."

They both turned toward the closed door and noticed a growing wet spot appearing on the carpet. Just as they got up to investigate, a small explosion sound came from outside the door and smoke began pouring from the rug, and almost instantly the rug burst into flames.

"Fire!" yelled Herbert Fritz, and he dashed for the door. The room filled with smoke as everyone jumped to his feet, and in a rather confused state, they unsuccessfully looked for something that might extinguish the fire.

Just a few seconds after the fire broke out at the dining room, Mamah noticed a noise – as if something had been splashed against the door to the breakfast room. Just as she rose, the sound of the exploding fire startled her. Fingers of fire shot under the bottom of the door, and immediately the gasoline-soaked carpet erupted in flames. The room quickly filled with smoke and John and Martha began screaming.

Herbert Fritz ran toward the hallway but the flames were too intense. He turned and ran for the outside door at the other side of the room. It was locked! "Damn, someone help me break this door down!" he shouted. He threw his full weight against it trying to break it open, but he finally gave up and threw his body against the window next to the door. The glass shattered and he fell to the ground outside five feet below. When he landed he felt his right arm snap and he was knocked nearly unconscious. As he lay there trying to get his bearings, Mr. Brodelle came flying through the window, and then William Weston right behind him.

Julian Carlton heard the window break. He ran around the end of the building just as Brodelle came through the window.

Stunned, Herbert shook his head and focused on the horrifying scene that unfolded before him. Julian Carlton came running around the corner, struck Mr. Brodelle with the hatchet, then turned and hit William Weston in the head with a devastating blow. Weston fell to the ground, but he got to his feet again and staggered across the lawn to the studio. Carlton followed him and struck him a second time.

While Carlton was chasing Weston, Herbert Fritz got up and staggered to a hiding spot behind the garden shed. He stayed there for a minute and then made his way around to the side of the house where he found Weston bleeding but able to walk. Although both were seriously injured, they managed to get away and hurried the best they could down the road to the neighbor's house about half a mile away.

"What the hell has gotten into Julian?" Weston gasped as they ran. He was bleeding from two gashes in his head where Carlton had struck him with the hatchet.

"He's gone berserk. He must have started the fire, too," Fritz responded. "We'd better hurry or he'll kill them all."

Carlton returned to the hallway door and waited. In a few seconds, through the fire and smoke David Lindblom crashed through what was left of the door with his clothes on fire. He staggered out into the hallway, and a second later he fell dead to a violent blow from Carlton's deadly hatchet. Right behind him, young Ernie Weston ran screaming from the room, his clothes nearly burned off. Carlton knocked him down with the first blow, and as Ernie lay there stunned, Carlton struck him several more times with the hatchet. Ernie died where he fell.

Thomas Brunker was nearly unconscious from the smoke, but with his last ounce of strength he managed to crawl through the door into the hallway. He saw Lindblom and Ernie Weston lying there with the bloody wounds on their heads. He had only just a second to be afraid. Carlton delivered a skull-splitting blow, and he was dead instantly.

With his murderous deed done to the men, Julian turned to Mamah and the children who were just down the hall.

Mamah Borthwick grabbed a cloth napkin from the breakfast table, wrapped it around the red-hot doorknob, and managed to get the door open. "Come children," she screamed. "We have to get out of here!" But before she could get through the doorway, Carlton's hatchet found its mark, this time in Mamah's forehead. John and Martha, screaming with terror saw their mother fall backward into the room. Martha's dress caught fire and she darted toward her only choice to escape the flames – the hallway door. But Carlton ended her flight, and her life. She lay in the hallway with her clothes burning.

Carlton could see little John in the room, but the flames were too intense for him to reach the boy, and he retreated back down the hallway. Terrified, John tried to open the outside door but he found it locked. He was becoming hysterical. He had just witnessed the murder of his mother and sister, and now he was completely trapped by the raging fire. His screams for help went unanswered. He crawled under the table, trying to get away from the flames. He closed his eyes and cried. In just a short while, the terribly thick smoke overcame him, and a few minutes later the ceiling fell, crushing the table and little John. Soon the floor gave way and his body fell into the basement with the burning floorboards and beams and furniture, and was turned to ashes with the house.

Chapter 57

7:50 AM

Now, let us once again rejoin Ladd, Tone, and Willie, who have been sleeping soundly in the bunkhouse, and are yet unaware of the dastardly deeds of the disgruntled manservant, or that they are about to face grave danger.

"**A**hab, cut it out! Go away!" I pushed the dog away from my face. He was whining and scratching at me and jumping up on my bed. "Go pester Willie."

He barked loudly and repeatedly, as if demanding our attention. He jumped back up on the bed and barked some more. "Ahab, leave us alone, go..." The way Ahab was carrying on, I knew something had to be wrong and I opened my eyes. The room was full of smoke! "Tone! There's smoke! Tone wake up... fire!" I shouted as I sat up quickly. "Willie, get up! The house is on fire!"

Tone and I jumped out of the bed and slipped on our shorts. We were coughing and could hardly see each other because the smoke was getting thicker by the second. "Get down, Tone... on the floor," I yelled.

We hadn't yet heard any response from Willie, nor could we see if he was stirring at all because of the smoke. We crawled over to his bed and Tone stood up to shake him. "Willie! Willie! Wake up!" Tone grabbed Willie and he was as limp as a rag doll. "Oh God, Ladd! He's unconscious!"

"Get him down off of that top bunk. He's been breathing smoke a lot longer than we have. Let's get out of here."

I grabbed Ahab, and Tone carried Willie, and stooping as low as we could with burdens in our arms, we made our way across the floor to the doorway in the hall. I reached the door first and opened it, and more smoke billowed through the doorway into the room. We crawled out into the hallway and we could see fire coming out of the dining room and the breakfast room. As I entered the hallway I saw David Lindblom with his head all bashed in lying on the floor in a pool of blood. Mr. Carlton stood by the door to the dining room and I thought he was trying to help the men out to safety.

But just as I was about to yell to him for help, I saw Ernie Weston bolt through the dining room door with his clothes on fire, screaming for help. He fell onto the floor of the hallway, and I expected Julian to come to his aid, but instead, Julian Carlton raised his arm and that's when I saw the hatchet in his hand. He ruthlessly bashed Ernie in the head with the hatchet. Ernie dropped to the floor and lay there bleeding, silent and still.

I was so shocked by the sight that I didn't move. Suddenly I felt Tone pulling on my arm. He put his finger to his lips and motioned to the back door. "Let's go that way," he whispered. We crawled back into the bunkhouse and across the floor to the outside door. I pulled on the doorknob, but the door was locked. "Locked! Damn, we've gotta get out of here!" The smoke was getting so thick that we would soon be unable to breathe at all. I handed Ahab to Tone, crawled to the table, felt around until I found a chair, grabbed it and took a deep breath of air from close to the floor. I stood up and smashed the chair through the window glass. I climbed up on the windowsill and jumped to the ground. Tone lifted Willie over the sill and handed him down to me. A few seconds later Tone came sailing out the window with Ahab in his arms.

"Let's get out of sight in case Carlton comes looking for us," I said.

Tone took Willie in his arms again and we ran to the back of the main house. We stopped by the pond. Willie was blue and his tongue was lolling out the side of his mouth.

"Ladd! Willies not breathing!" Tone screamed.

"Oh God! No! Willie, come on, Willie! Breathe!" I shouted.

Tone slapped him and shook him and tried to revive him. "Willie, come on, kid. Breathe!"

Willie didn't respond. "I'm gonna try something," I said.

I laid Willie down on the ground, opened his mouth, put my mouth over his and blew into his lungs. His chest rose and fell. I blew again and again, and each time Willie's chest rose and fell as the breath filled his lungs and then escaped. Tone talked to him and rubbed his chest and arms. "Come on, Willie. Don't you leave us. Come on, little brother. Please, God, don't take him, please!" We were both in tears and were just about hysterical. I breathed another breath into Willie, and then another, and suddenly he began coughing. "That's it, breathe Willie!" Tone yelled. "Come on, you little shit. Breathe!"

Willie coughed again, laid still for a second or two, and inhaled a couple of big breaths on his own. His eyes fluttered open. They were full of tears from the smoke and when he batted his eyelids a couple of times, the tears streaked down his soot-covered face. "Little shit?" he mumbled.

"Willie! Thank God, thank God," I said, and hugged him tightly to my chest.

Tone threw his arms around Willie, too, and just about squeezed him to death between us. "If you guys don't let me up to breathe," came Willie's voice from between us, "I'm gonna suffocate!" We released our hold on him, he inhaled deeply again several times, and then he grinned. We all had tears streaming down, making streaks in the soot and grime from the fire. We had escaped tragedy, but most importantly, just then, our Willie was back.

Ahab began licking Willie's sooty face. Willie sat up and hugged the dog. "Ahab, you look a little black. What the heck happened?"

That's kind of what we were wondering too.

Chapter 58

The fire spread quickly; smoke seeped from the roof and then it burst into flames, and then some of the walls began falling in, and soon most of the house was burning. We stayed hidden, not knowing where Mr. Carlton was, and not wanting to take a chance on him coming after us with that hatchet. "Willie, I think Carlton set the house afire on purpose." I said.

"Why would he do that?"

"He must be crazy. We saw Mr. Lindblom with his head all smashed in, and while we were trying to get you out, he killed Ernie right in front of us. He was hiding outside the door with a hatchet and hit Ernie with it as he ran past. He *must* have gone crazy."

"Where are Mamah and John and Martha?" Willie asked.

We shook our heads. "We haven't seen anyone alive except Carlton and us."

The flames began shooting higher into the air and the heat became unbearable, so we moved farther from the house and hid by the pond. Soon cars began coming down the driveway and neighbors began to arrive to try to help. We saw Mr. Weston and Mr. Fritz get out of one of the cars. Mr. Weston had a bandage on his head and his clothes were drenched in blood. Mr. Fritz was cradling his arm as though it had been injured. When we saw them we ran out from behind the bushes. "My God, you boys made it out. Thank God!" Mr. Weston said. "Have you seen anyone else? Have you seen my son, Ernie?"

Bitter sadness engulfed Tone and he said to Mr. Weston, "I think Mr. Carlton killed Ernie, sir. We saw him with a bloody hatchet and found David Lindblom with his head all bashed in. The guy went nuts and killed everybody." Tone broke down and began crying.

Mr. Weston's eyes filled with tears. "No one else is alive... just Fritz and the four of us? My God, he's killed seven people! What

199

the hell got into him?"

Just then the sheriff drove up and Mr. Weston and Mr. Fritz began telling him what had happened. The Spring Green fire brigade was on the way, but it would be too little, too late, as much of the house was already destroyed.

The sheriff questioned us and we told him what we had seen. He wrote it all down. Finally the fire brigade arrived and began pumping water from the pond onto the house. It was a lost cause, but after a couple of hours they did finally manage to put the fire out. We stood by and tried to stay out of the way, all the while keeping an eye out for Mr. Carlton.

A large crowd had gathered, and women began setting up tables and putting out food for the men who were fighting the fire, and those who were attempting to locate the bodies. The three of us must have looked pretty pitiful, too – Tone and I had our shorts on and nothing else, and poor Willie only had his underwear left. We were all covered with soot and grime. Several of the ladies brought us sandwiches and lemonade.

After some time they began carrying out the bodies. We saw them carry out Ernie and Mrs. Borthwick and Martha. All three were terribly burned and had awful wounds on their heads.

"Where is John?" Willie asked.

"We haven't seen any sign of him yet," the fireman said sadly shaking his head.

Then they carried out Mr. Lindblom and Mr. Brunker and finally the body of Mr. Brodelle. The bodies of the four men and Mamah and little Martha were all laid in the grass and covered with sheets. A while later one of the men came out and talked quietly to the sheriff. He walked back into the burned house, and in a short while he returned carrying a very small body wrapped in a blanket. The sheriff came to us and said; "They found little John, what's left of him, in the basement. I'm real sorry."

Willie couldn't hold back the tears. He buried his face in Ahab's fur and cried. We left him to his grief for a while, and then we asked the sheriff if it would be all right for us to leave for home. There was nothing but horror to see if we stayed any longer. The sheriff took our names and addresses and said that if he needed us to testify against Mr. Carlton, he would contact us, but he didn't think that would be likely, as long as Mr. Weston and Mr. Fritz were there.

"We haven't found Carlton yet, but I'm sure we will," he said.

We said goodbye to Mr. Fritz and told Mr. Weston that we were sorry for the loss of his son, Ernie. "He was a real nice kid," Tone said. "I think we'd be good friends if we could have had the time to know him better."

Mr. Weston thanked us and we walked solemnly down the path to the river. Our boat was right where we had left it, and it surely would take us to happier places.

Chapter 59

We untied the boat and turned it over. All of our blankets, some canned food, and our tarp for making a shelter were still under it. The rest of our clothes had burned up so all we had was what we were wearing. Tone and I lifted Voyageur off the dock and down onto the riverbank, slid it into the water, and we all pitched in to load the gear. Tone sat in the front seat, Willie sat down in the middle, forlorn and holding Ahab in his arms, and I took the rear. We pushed off into the current.

None of us felt much like talking, so we just paddled toward our homes in the west. Willie sat with his back against the side of the boat and his legs stretched across to the other side. He just stared at the river as we paddled along. We had gone only four or five miles, but my concern for his well-being overwhelmed me. I thought it might be a good idea to stop for a while.

"Are you okay, Willie?" I asked.

He nodded, but didn't say anything. I could plainly see his wet eyes, but he hid his face in his hands and tried not to let me see him crying.

"Tone. Head over to that sandbar," I said.

We pulled up on the sandbar. I got out, sat on the edge of the boat and put my arm around Willie. "It's okay, Willie. It's okay to cry. That was a terrible thing we went through."

Tone sat on the other side of Willie and put his arm around him, too. "Hey, little brother. It's gonna be all right. We're all safe now."

Willie cried like a baby and we held him for a long time. The sun was getting low on the horizon, so I suggested that we camp right there for the night. Tone waded across a narrow, shallow channel to the riverbank and found some firewood while Willie and I turned the boat on its side and arranged our shelter. We built a fire and heated some canned beef and a can of beans for supper.

Although we were pretty short on clothes, it was still warm and comfortable even after the sun went down. We just sat quietly between the fire and the upturned boat and stared into the flames, and for a long time no one spoke.

"Do you guys believe in God?" Willie asked after the long silence.

I glanced at Tone, caught a little off-guard with the question. "I guess I do, Willie. We don't do a lot of church-going, but I think He's there someplace."

"Me too, Willie," Tone said. "You might not remember because you were unconscious, but when Ladd was breathing into your lungs, I was praying to God to give you back to us."

"Give me back? You mean... I was dead?"

"Well, you weren't breathing for a while. I guess maybe that means you were dead, but I don't know for sure."

Willie sat for a long time again without saying a word. Finally he said, "I remember seeing John – at least I think I saw him. He was wearing white shorts and a white shirt and he kind of had this glow around him. He was in this place that was all kind of dark and cloudy, but it wasn't a bad place. It seemed kind of peaceful. John was up above me and he was calling to me."

"Jeez, Willie. Are you sure?"

"I... well... that's what I remember. He was smiling and he waved to me and he said, 'Willie, your daddy is waiting for you.' Then I could hear someone calling to me, 'Don't leave us, Willie, come back.'"

"Wow! That's spooky," Tone said.

"I can remember it pretty clear. But it wasn't scary. It was kind of a nice place, actually."

"Then what happened?" I asked.

"Well... John smiled at me and said it again, 'Your daddy is waiting for you, Willie,' and then he waved goodbye to me and turned, and he kind of... like... just evaporated."

We were all rather speechless at that point. Tone and I both put our arms around Willie and held him tight between us. We sat for a long time just feeling very lucky that Willie was still with us.

After another long silence, Tone finally said, "Ladd, I've been meaning to ask you, but with all the excitement I kept forgetting. How did you know to breathe into Willie's lungs like that?"

"I saw my grandpa do it when one of his cows dropped a calf that wasn't breathing. He cleaned all the gooey crap out of its mouth and put his mouth over its nose and mouth and blew his breath in, and the calf started breathing. I remembered seeing that, and I guess I thought it was worth a try to save Willie."

"You put your lips on mine? Arrrgggghhh, I'm poisoned!" Willie wheezed, falling to his side and shaking like a dying chicken.

"It's not like I wanted to marry you, Willie," I said laughing.

Willie scrubbed his lips with the back of his hand, spat several times, and then grinned at me, his teeth shining white amidst his soot blackened face.

"Now, there's our old Willie back, good as new," Tone said, laughing.

Willie sat up and laughed, too. "I guess this means I have to be your slave for life."

"Yeah, right, Willie! You just grow up and have a long, good life, and that'll be enough payment for me."

Willie hugged me, and then he hugged Tone. "Thanks for looking after me."

We decided to turn in for the night. We laid one of the blankets on the sand under the middle of the tarp, and we all snuggled in together. Willie smiled as he slid between Tone and me and pulled another blanket over all of us. Ahab worked his way up under the blanket and nestled in by Willie's feet. Tonight at least, Willie was the safest boy in the world.

Chapter 60

The sun was high in the sky before we began to stir the next morning. The previous day had taken a lot out of us and it was good to lie there feeling the warmth of my two best friends next to me. This would be our last day on the river, and probably the last day of the summer that we'd spend together. I wanted it to last as long as we could make it last.

Willie was nestled against Tone's shoulder with his mouth hanging open, snoring quietly. His face and hair was still streaked with soot. He began stirring, opened his eyes and saw me next to him. "Are you watching me sleep?" he said, yawning.

"I was just awake and thinking," I replied.

Tone rolled over, rubbing his sleepy eyes. "I slept like a log. Man, I didn't know how exhausted I was until I laid down last night."

Nestled down by Tone's feet, Ahab yawned and stretched. "Ahab kept my feet nice and warm, too," Tone chuckled.

"Thanks for letting me sleep between you guys," Willie said. "It was a safe feeling for me."

"You're welcome, little buddy," Tone answered, and then with a bit of sarcasm he said, "now go start a fire and fetch us some breakfast, will you?"

Willie punched Tone's arm, and Tone tickled him, and soon we were all rolling and laughing. In the free-for-all, one of the paddles got kicked out from under the boat and it fell over on top of us. Ahab barked joyously and jumped onto the heap, too, thinking it was a great game. We wrestled and kept tickling Willie until he screamed for mercy. Suddenly, there was a terrible stink under the boat.

"Willie! You nasty little thing!"

"Wasn't me. It was Ahab!" Willie laughed. "Ahab! Bad dog!"

We laughed until we cried as we attempted to untangle each other and get the boat off of us. "Whew! Fresh air," I said as I crawled from under the boat.

Surveying our dirty, sooty bodies, I suggested that we all needed a bath. There didn't seem to be any objections, and we took off our grimy shorts and jumped into the river with our bar of soap. The morning had warmed up quite nicely, and the bath was quite refreshing after such a rough day. When we were all squeaky clean again, Tone and Willie made a fire while I tried to wash the soot and grime out of our shorts and Willie's underwear. They were the only clothes we had left. I hung them over one edge of the boat to dry while we ate some of the last of our food. There wasn't much left – some stale bread, a few cans of beans, and a jar of grape jam.

By the time we tipped the boat upright and packed up our gear, our shorts weren't quite dry, but it really didn't matter. We put them on anyway, and shoved *Voyageur* off the sandbar, into the westward current.

This river was the river we knew. *Our* river was broad and flat and full of islands and sandbars. The water was shallow, and clear and the bottom was sandy. It was so much different than the narrow, deep, dark colored channels upriver that flowed fast and hard, and where the bottom was mostly rock and gravel. It was hard to imagine that this was still the same river.

"Now this is more what we're used to," I said.

"Yeah, I was just thinking that, too," Tone said as he looked over his shoulder.

"Someday we should take a trip from home down to the Mississippi," Willie said jubilantly.

"Maybe next summer, Willie."

After several hours of steady paddling, we stopped for a rest on a sandbar to get the kinks out of our legs and stretch a bit. We were on the last leg of our journey home when, late in the afternoon, Willie shouted, "I can see the church steeple! Look! D'ya see it?"

He was pointing to the left above the trees. Sure enough, there was the steeple of *St. John the Baptist* church, the tallest building in town.

"We'll be home in less than half an hour," I said.

Although we were all quite excited and anxious to tell everyone about our great adventure, I think we all felt a little sad, too, that it was just about at its end.

Chapter 61

Wearing nothing but cut-off shorts that were faded and looking pretty ragged, and Willie in just his underwear that was full of holes and the color of muddy water, we must have been quite a sight as we walked down the street. Tone's dark curly hair had grown to shoulder length and his skin was so dark he could have passed for a native from some tropical island.

Willie's hair, and mine, too, was nearly to our shoulders and had sun bleached to a white blonde color. We weren't as dark as Tone, but we were both quite darkly tanned from head to toe. We got a lot of stares as we passed our neighbors' houses, but when we waved and said hello, they realized who we really were, and they smiled and returned the greeting.

When we turned the corner at the Funeral Home, we saw an automobile parked in the street in front of Willie's house.

"Holy smokes! Who do you know who has a motor car?" I asked Willie.

"Beats me. The only motorcars I've ever seen were up north. I don't know anybody who actually owns one."

We could hear what sounded like quite a party going on in the back yard, so we headed around the side of the house. Much to our surprise, Tone's parents were there, my parents were there, and among a few other neighbors and friends, Mr. DeSilva was there, too, all joined with Willie's mom and sisters around several tables filled with food and drinks for a wonderful looking picnic.

"Willie!" his mom yelled when she saw us.

"There they are! They're back!" everyone shouted and crowded around us.

Our families hugged us and everyone was talking at once. They urged us to sit at a table and the moms started piling more food in front of us than we could possibly eat. All the while everyone had a hundred questions about our trip. But of course, we had to tell our dads how well *Voyageur* performed, first.

There was one man sitting with his back to us at the far table. He looked familiar from the back, and then he turned around and gave me a big grin.

"Harvey! Hey, Tone, Willie... Harvey's here, too!"

We all got up and ran to greet Harvey Honer, who was mysteriously sitting in Willie's back yard with our families. Tone and I shook his hand, and then he knelt down and greeted Willie with a bone-crushing hug. "Young Willie! How was your adventure?"

"Harvey? You're not gonna believe it."

We sat down again, and everyone was talking to us at once while we ate ravenously. The meager food that we had eaten the past day and a half was not enough for us to really get full, but now that was not a problem. We had foods that we hadn't seen all summer, and they tasted fantastic.

"Whose automobile is that out there?" I asked.

Harvey grinned. "I got tired of taking six days from Wausau to here, so I bought it the day you boys left on your quest. I've been here for the last week."

"Why are you here, Harvey?" Willie asked. "Not that we aren't glad to see you, but you couldn't have brought any caskets in that motorcar... did you?"

Harvey smiled and put his arm around Willie's mother. "Your mom and I have something to tell you, Willie."

Chapter 62

I gazed at my mom and dad and they were wearing big smiles, and Tone's parents were beaming, too. What the heck was going on? The three of us sat down on a bench and waited.

"I think I'd better start at the beginning," Harvey said. "Do you boys remember last year when you first helped unload caskets?"

Harvey probably wasn't looking for a response, but we all nodded anyway.

"Well," he went on, but talking more directly to Willie. "That day Mr. DeSilva and I went up town for some... hmmm... throat soothing medicine, and we talked about many things. He mentioned that your father had been killed when you were very young, and that your mother had worked so hard to keep you and your sisters fed and clothed. I thought that was a wonderful thing, and after we had paid you boys and you went home, I stopped here to introduce myself, and I asked your mom if she would allow me to help her out. She didn't want to take charity, but I offered it in friendship, and we did become very good friends. But it has grown to more than just that in the past year. We wrote letters back and forth, and the past few times I've been here delivering caskets, we've met and had dinner, and really got to know each other.

"You see, Willie, I've been very lucky in life as far as my

business goes. My company makes a quality product, and I make a very good living. But money isn't everything, and when I lost my wife, and then my son, I was left with a huge house and no one to share it with."

I glanced toward Willie. He was spellbound, listening to Harvey.

"When you boys left Wausau the other day, I had a telegram waiting for me at the office. It was from the Department of the Army. They offered me a contract to build caskets for the Army in preparation for the time when we will most likely go to war in Europe. And, while I detest the idea of making profit from war, they convinced me that I would be doing the country a service by providing quality caskets for our fallen soldiers. I accepted the contract, but my factory in Wausau isn't large enough to do the work, so I've decided to build a new factory."

Harvey smiled and pointed to the two men sitting across the table. "And Eric and Robert are going to run it for me."

Tone gasped. "Does that mean we're moving to Wausau?"

"No, the new factory will be built right here in Muscoda," my dad said. "And it'll provide jobs for twenty five or thirty workers."

"Your fathers will be managers, and they can still build houses if they want to. In fact, I've already made a contract with them to build me a new house, right over there." He pointed to a vacant lot down the street.

This was all too much, too fast. "Wait a minute," Willie interrupted. "What about your factory in Wausau?"

"My foreman will run it, and I'm going to keep my home there, too. We can go up there on the weekends and vacations... whenever we feel like it."

"We? Who's we?"

"Your mother, your sisters, you, and me," Harvey said. "And Tone and Ladd and their families, too, if they want to see the North Country."

Willie was completely baffled. He stared questioningly at

Tone and me a few moments, and we just shrugged our shoulders. We had no idea of what was going on, either.

Harvey put his arm around Willie's mom and smiled. "Willie, I've asked your mother to marry me, and she said 'yes.'"

Willie turned to me and Tone with a dumbfounded, strange expression accented with tears. "John said my daddy is waiting for me."

A chill tingled my spine. "He was right, Willie. Your daddy *is* waiting for you, right here. Your *new* daddy."

Willie jumped up and threw his arms around Harvey's neck, and if he hadn't been such a skinny little guy, he might have choked him to death. There wasn't a dry eye in the entire back yard.

"Who is John?" I heard someone say.

Chapter 63

After Harvey's news sank in, mass chatter started again. Everybody was hugging each other, celebrating the good fortune that was coming to us all. Tone and I hugged Willie for reasons that none of the others would understand, right then. Then, as if she had just noticed, Willie's mom scolded, "My Lord, Willie. You're nearly naked! Where are your clothes?"

Willie shot me a warning glare and said, "Ah... the boat tipped over, Ma, and I lost them. We lost all our shirts and extra stuff, and my shorts, too."

"Good Lord. Well, run in the house and wash up, and get some clothes on," she ordered.

"We're gonna run home and clean up, too," I said, noticing that everyone else was all dressed up, and Tone and I were in tattered shorts and nothing else.

"Come right back," Harvey said, grinning like a fox. "I have one more surprise for you."

We ran home, took quick baths and put on clean shorts, shirts and shoes. It felt strange wearing shoes for the first time in many weeks. By the time we got back, Willie was all clean and changed into some new cut off bib overalls. That was it – no shirt, and no shoes – standard Willie attire until school started.

Harvey sat us down and said, "One of the things that I think is most important in life is a good education. The more advanced our country becomes, the more an education is necessary for a good life. It took me a while to convince your fathers to work for me. They are artisans in their craft, and I had to convince them that this is work that is necessary for our country."

Tone and I exchanged curious glances. We weren't sure just what Harvey was building up to.

"The clincher that finally convinced them to accept my offer," he continued, "was my proposal that I will pay for your university education as a benefit of their employment with my company. They agreed, so next year when you boys graduate from high school, choose the university you wish to attend; I'll pay for it."

Tone and I were speechless. Neither of us had ever dreamed that we would have the opportunity to go to a university. "Harvey, I... I... I don't know what to say," I stammered.

"Harvey... Harvey..." Tone couldn't do any better.

Harvey gave a hearty laugh and put his arms around our shoulders. "You are two of the brightest lads I've ever known, and you have two of the best hearts I've ever seen. It makes me feel good to do it for you."

"But it must cost a huge lot of money," I said.

"Remember what you boys asked me when we were on the way to my house in Wausau?" Harvey smiled as he asked us the question.

I thought a moment. "Yeah. Willie asked if you were a mil...."

Harvey winked. "Don't worry about the money, boys."

The picnic went on into the evening and when it began to get dark we lit lanterns, and more neighbors came over to join in the festivities. Mr. DeSilva played his accordion and there was dancing and singing. Long after dark, Harvey got a box of fireworks from his automobile and we shot off rockets and streamers into the night. It was almost better than the Fourth of July.

Tone and Willie and I found ourselves sitting together on a bench near the back fence as the night wore on. "Let's just not say anything about Mr. Wright and all that," Willie said.

"I think that's a good idea, Willie. No need to make our moms all scared about something that's over and done with."

"We'll just let it be our secret, Willie." Tone wrapped his arm around Willie's shoulder.

The three of us sat there side-by-side, just as we had done so many times that summer. We watched our families celebrate. Willie's eyes hardly ever strayed from Harvey, and his smile was as big as Montana all the while he watched his new daddy.

"It's been quite a day," I said

"It's been quite a summer."

Chapter 64

For the first time in over two months, I woke up in my own bed. It was also the first time in two months that Tone and Willie weren't there. I lay there a few minutes reflecting on the past summer. There had been so many different experiences that I found it hard to concentrate on any single one. I got up out of bed, pulled on my shorts, and peered out my window. There was Tone, looking out his window, grinning like a Cheshire cat. "What's for breakfast?" he yelled across the yard.

"Don't know, but come on over. I'm quite sure Mom will make us *something*."

I ran downstairs. Mom was in the kitchen. "Mornin,' Ma. Can Tone come over for breakfast?"

"Isn't he already..."

Tone came through the door with a big smile.

"...On his way?" Mom finished.

"Good morning, Second Ma."

"Good morning, handsome. God, you get better looking every day. If I was twenty years younger...."

"Ma! Jeez!" I scolded.

Tone hugged her.

"You guys sit and have some cinnamon rolls while I fix the eggs."

The frying pan had just hit the stove when we heard a quiet little knock at the back door. Mom walked to the hallway and I heard her say, "Well, now we've got all three of you. How do you like your eggs, Sweetie?"

Willie came into the kitchen following Mom, smiling from ear to ear. "I like them any way you want to cook them, ma'am."

Mom hugged him and kissed him on top of the head. "It's so nice to have all our boys back home safe and sound."

"Hey, Willie. How did it feel to sleep in your own bed again?" Tone asked.

"It was okay... but I missed you guys when I woke up."

We all grinned. Somehow we knew that we had all been thinking the same thing.

"So, I think today we should take the boat down and pick up the rest of the stuff from the cabin," I suggested as I buttered a cinnamon roll.

"Good idea," Willie replied. "Anything to get me out of the house and away from my sisters."

Mom set a big platter of scrambled eggs and bacon on the table. It disappeared in short order. "I'll have to go to the market more often now that you're home," she laughed.

Mom told us that Dad and Robert were staking out Harvey's new house. So when we finished breakfast, the three of us strolled to his building lot. Harvey, Dad, and Robert were there driving stakes into the ground and stringing cords between them to lay out the house so they could start digging the basement. They were referring to some drawings on a big sheet of paper that gave the basic dimensions and plan for the house.

"Hey, there's our intrepid river explorers," Harvey joyously announced as we walked up. "What are you lads doing today?"

"We're getting our stuff from the cabin and close it up for the winter," I said. "Want to come and see it?"

"I think that would be a grand idea," Harvey exclaimed. "We're about done here anyway." He handed the big paper to Robert. "So, you think you can draw up some plans for me?"

"Yes, I'm sure I can," Robert replied.

"Ladd," Tone said to me. "You and Willie take Harvey to the cabin. I think I'll look at these plans with Dad. I have some ideas that I'd like to suggest."

"Okay, if that's all right with everyone."

Tone's dad nodded, as if pleasantly surprised.

"Let's go, Harvey."

We walked leisurely down to the river as Harvey took in all the sights of the town that he would soon be calling home. Willie and I slid *Voyageur* into the water. Harvey sat in the middle on the picnic hamper and Willie took the front paddle. We made good time going downriver, and when we arrived at the island, we showed Harvey around.

"You boys made quite a place for yourselves here," he said. "There's just one thing I was wondering about that has me a bit confused."

"What's that, Harvey?" Willie asked.

"Well, yesterday you told us that you lost all of your extra clothes when the boat tipped over, yet here you have the picnic basket, your blankets, and the pots and pans. How is it that they didn't get lost when your clothes did?"

"Well, um..." I stalled, trying to formulate an answer.

"How about the truth? And by the way... I noticed that look you gave Tone and Ladd yesterday, young Willie."

"Promise you won't tell Ma?" Willie pleaded.

"Promise."

"They burned up in the fire," Willie said.

"The camp fire?"

"No, the fire at Mr. Wright's house."

Harvey's eyes widened. "You were at Taliesin when it burned? When that man murdered all those people?"

Willie nodded.

"My God! What happened?"

I began telling Harvey about how we met Mr. Wright when Willie saved his hat, and about the beams, and how we woke up to a room full of smoke, and found Willie not breathing. "If you hadn't told us about your son, we probably would have died in the smoke, but Tone remembered what you said, and we crawled out on the floor and we took Willie out with us."

"Willie wasn't breathing?"

I struggled with the memory, getting quite emotional just remembering the event. "He was looking awful peaked, and by the time we got him outside he had turned blue. So I blew into his lungs and he started breathing again. I had seen my grandpa do that to a calf, and it worked on Willie, too."

Harvey hands were shaking as we told him about seeing Mr. Carlton striking the others with the hatchet. He pulled Willie into his arms and hugged him so hard that Willie began to moan. "You're gonna crush me, Harvey," he mumbled from beneath Harvey's big arms.

Harvey released him and laughed. "My Lord. You nearly perish in a fire and escape the hatchet of a madman and here I am crushing you to death."

He held my shoulders with his strong hands and looked me right in the eyes. "I'll always be grateful to you for saving Willie. I don't know if I could have stood to lose another son." He put his arms around me and hugged me hard.

Willie's eyes got big when he heard that. He took Harvey's big hand in his. "Harvey? Is it okay if I start calling you Pa?"

"I think I'd like that a lot, Willie. I truly would."

We loaded up the rest of our gear and bid the cabin farewell. Harvey paddled on the way upriver, as Willie's little arms didn't have enough power to move us along against the current. When we got to the landing where we usually left the boat, we pulled it up on the sand.

"I'll get Tone and the wagon," I said. "We'll take it home and put it away."

We walked together as far as where I turned to go to my house, and I bid Harvey and Willie goodbye. Willie took Harvey's hand. "See ya later, Ladd," he said over his shoulder, and they walked together down the street toward his house.

"Later," I answered.

I watched as they walked; a big man and a little boy, hand in hand, and as happy as they could be. I heard Willie say, "Now remember, Pa. You promised you won't tell Ma about me almost being dead."

"Yes, young Willie. I'll keep my promise."

Chapter 65

D uring the next few weeks, Dad and Robert hired a gang of helpers and Harvey's new house began to take shape. When Robert and Tone showed Harvey the plans, he was quite impressed. Tone had done much of the work, and had added some unique features.

"So you are telling me that this will just stick out of the front wall with no support?" Harvey asked.

"It's called a cantilever;" Tone said. "It's supported by piers that are built into the wall, and it ties into the floor inside. We can put a roof over it and a wall of windows. Then in the winter, it'll act as a heat collector and it can be used to grow plants, just like a hothouse. And in the summer the windows can be exchanged for screens, and it'll be a great porch for sitting in the evening."

"I like it, Tone," Harvey said. "Let's do it."

Tone winked at Willie and me. We knew where he had gotten the idea for the cantilever.

The basement was built and the entire house was roughed in before winter came so the finish work inside could be done during the cold weather. Tone and Willie and I helped on weekends, as the house gradually became a magnificent home. There would be none finer in the whole town.

Plans for the casket factory were going along as scheduled, too. Harvey bought land on the other side of town near other factories. He figured to start construction as soon as his new house was finished. Dad and Robert and their crew would build it, and many of the helpers had already been promised jobs when the factory opened.

Then one day in March, when the house was nearly done, Mom and Dad and I were eating breakfast in our kitchen when we heard an automobile horn in the driveway – Aooogah, Aooogah. I ran to the door, and there, in our driveway sat a new auto with a big red bow on its windshield. "Mom, Dad, come here!" I shouted.

We all hurried out into the spring sunshine and noticed that Tone and his family were out in their yard staring at an identical motorcar. "What the heck's going on?" I yelled to Tone. He shrugged his shoulders.

Just then Harvey and Willie pulled into the yard in Harvey's auto. Willie had a mile-wide grin on his face. "Good morning, good morning! What a splendid day it is," Harvey greeted us all.

"Harvey, what's this all about?" Dad said.

"Whatever do you mean?" Harvey said, his eyes just twinkling.

By then, Robert, Angela, and Tone had joined us.

"I mean where did these two autos come from?"

"Why, I suppose from Mr. Ford's auto factory," Harvey said, and laughed uproariously at his own joke. "Willie, tell the folks about the autos, will you?"

Willie beamed and giggled like one of his little sisters. "Pa thought that since the casket factory is all the way on the other side of town, his partners should have motorcars so they can get back and forth easier."

Dad and Robert were stunned. "What do you mean? Partners," Robert asked.

"I've determined that there is going to be much work here; caskets, building houses, and I'm thinking we might even have a furniture division. I can't possibly keep track of all that, so you are now legally one third owners of Muscoda Furniture and Casket Company, and equal partners of Muscoda Builders."

Willie giggled uncontrollably, and Harvey beamed with pride and satisfaction. The rest of us stood there with our mouths gaping.

"Harvey... we don't know what to say," Dad muttered.

"Just say 'yes, you'll accept my offer.'"

"Yes, I accept." Dad said, reaching for Harvey's hand.

"Yes, Harvey. Yes!" Robert confirmed.

"The papers have all been drawn up by my lawyer. All we have to do is sign them, and we're in business."

There were handshakes and hugs all around, and then we all went into our house and celebrated with a big family breakfast for the whole gang. Later, we all gathered in the living room and it seemed like everyone was talking at once. Willie squeezed in between Tone and me on the couch. He put his arms around our shoulders and grinned. "I not only got a new Pa... now I've got two whole new families, too."

After so many years of struggling and just getting by, all of our families were looking at a bright, new future.

Chapter 66

Willie's new house was finished in April. Dad and Robert had made cabinets and furniture, and an army of painters, wallpaper hangers, and decorators worked for weeks finishing the inside.

We were spending more time with Willie's family now, and Tone and I became pretty friendly with his two oldest sisters, Ellie and Frannie. Ellie was the oldest and was the same age as Tone and me. She was really pretty with dark brown hair, deep blue eyes, and a perpetual smile. She and I enjoyed our time we spent together regularly.

Frannie was the lively one – blonde hair, green eyes, a few freckles across her nose, and a hearty laugh. Tone always seemed to be close to her whenever we picnicked or went somewhere together. Of course, every chance Willie had, he was playing matchmaker.

"As much as I can't stand those stupid girls," he said, "I'd be real happy if you married my sisters and got them out of the house." He grinned. "Besides... then we'd be *real* brothers, or at least brothers-in-law."

The big wedding – Harvey and Willie's mom – was about one month off and all of the women were busy getting ready for it. Willie's two oldest sisters, my mom and Angela were to be bridesmaids, and Dad, Robert, Tone and I were groomsmen. Willie's other sisters were to be the flower girl and maid of honor. Willie was the best man.

Harvey made an appointment with a tailor. We all piled into our motorcars and traveled to Richland Center to be measured and fitted for our new formal wear for the wedding – light gray trousers, dark gray pinstriped formal coats with long tails in the back, white shirts, red bow ties, and shiny new black shoes.

When we each had tried on the coat and trousers, and the tailor had chalked and pinned them for a perfect fit, we were ready for the trip back home. Someone would come back in four weeks to pick up the finished suits.

The women would wear long satin dresses, all different colors with big bows on the back, and long white gloves. Willie's mom had a magnificent wedding gown made of lace and embroidery with a long veil that trailed behind her.

They spent hours planning the wedding dinner and dance that would follow, and fussed over everything else right down to the most minute detail.

The men got haircuts and made sure their fingernails were clean.

When the big day finally came, everyone was excited and just a little nervous. We all met at the church; Dad, Robert, Tone and I sat in the front pew in the proper order, like we had practiced. But Willie was nowhere in sight. "He'll be along soon," Harvey said. "He was griping about the shirt choking him and the shoes hurting his feet when I left."

I poked Dad in the ribs. "Did you see? Mr. DeSilva wasn't about to be outdone by anyone," I whispered. "He bought a motorcar, too. I saw him parking it right next to ours."

The church filled with people. It was just about time to start and Willie hadn't shown up yet. "Where do you suppose that little shit is?" Tone whispered to me.

"Little shit?" Willie whispered as he snuck in from the side aisle and sat next to me.

"We thought you might have gone fishing."

Willie just grinned. He pulled at his collar and acted as if he were choking. "I'm gonna die in this thing," he complained.

I adjusted his tie. "You look very handsome, Willie. Just be patient, and remember – this is your mom's big day."

He fidgeted and wiggled constantly for the few minutes before the ceremony began. The organ started playing and Mom walked slowly down the aisle. When she got to the front of the church, Dad joined her and they went to the front and split to the right and the left. Then Angela came down the aisle and Robert met her and they followed Dad and Mom.

Frannie was next in line, and Tone winked at me when she was almost to the front. "Wow, Ladd, look at her. She's beautiful."

"Go get her, tiger," I whispered.

Tone had a big smile on his face as he and Frannie met and they stepped to their places.

Next came Ellie, and she was gorgeous, too. She nearly took my breath away as she came closer.

Willie poked me. "Your turn, Romeo."

I winked, stepped into the aisle, met Ellie, and we took our places with the others.

Willie's littlest sister came up the aisle dropping flower petals on the long white cloth on the floor, and then his youngest sister came up the aisle. They met and took their places in the front.

The organist played a fanfare and then the strains of *Here Comes the Bride* flowed from the choir loft. Willie's mom looked like a queen as she floated down the aisle in the magnificent gown. When she reached the front of the church, Harvey stepped out from the sacristy and joined her in front of the priest.

The music stopped and Father Surges began the ceremony. Everyone was smiling and very happy, and the vows and everything else went just as we had rehearsed. Then the Priest asked for the rings. Willie reached into his pocket, took them out, and handed the rings, tied together with a ribbon, to the Father Surges. He looked pretty pleased that he had accomplished his job flawlessly.

The Priest blessed the rings and handed the large one to Willie's mom. She spoke her vow and put the ring on Harvey's finger. Father Surges handed Harvey the other ring. Harvey must have been a little nervous; he dropped it. He stooped over to pick it up and stopped abruptly. He began laughing uproariously, and every one in the church craned their necks to see what was going on. Harvey glanced toward Tone and me and pointed to Willie's feet.

Of course, Willie was barefoot. Well, it *was* summer, wasn't it?

Epilog

Five Years Later

Times have been quite good for our families since that spring day when Harvey married Willie's mom.

The Muscoda Casket and Furniture Company flourished. As the war began to wind down, the Company converted more and more of its workforce to the production of fine furniture. Dad and Robert both built wonderful new houses next door to Harvey's. The Muscoda Construction Company has gained fame as a builder of great homes and is busier than ever.

Tone and I graduated from high school and went to the university, just as Harvey had promised us, and we shared an apartment during our years together there.

Tone earned his degree in Architecture; now he designs most of the homes and some of the furniture for the Company. One of his favorite designs is the cantilever, and he uses it often in his home designs.

I earned my degree in Marketing. I'm in charge of advertising and community relations for the Company, and I spend a lot of my time laying out catalogs and writing ads. Tone and I share a large office.

I married Ellie and Tone married Frannie in a double ring ceremony, right after we graduated from the university. Willie was best man for both of us. When Dad and Mom and Tone's parents moved into their new homes, Tone and I took over our boyhood homes, next door to each other. Ellie and Frannie are both expecting babies next fall, and as close as we can tell, their due dates are two days apart.

Willie has matured from a cute, skinny little kid into a strikingly handsome young man. He's as tall as Tone and me, and he's never lost that twinkle in those green eyes, or that perpetual grin. He and Harvey are nearly inseparable.

Willie has finally noticed girls and has decided that they

aren't so "yucky" as he once thought they were. And they have surely noticed him, too. He has no trouble finding a date for any occasion, and at a party or any kind of gathering, the girls are hanging all over him, much to his delight. He's still the funny kid that we've always known, and everyone just loves him.

We knew that Willie had an exceptional talent for woodcarving, and as the furniture business expanded, Harvey, remembering the beautiful job he had done on *Voyageur,* provided him with the proper tools and asked Willie to begin working on some carvings. Now his intricate carvings are displayed on some of the finest furniture that the Company builds. He'll be attending the university this coming fall to study Art.

But we still have a hard time getting him to wear a shirt and shoes during the summer. Often, when Tone and I go to his workroom at the furniture factory to talk to him, or to pick him up for lunch, we find him working barefoot and shirtless.

Ahab became a proud papa when he got together with the neighbor's female beagle a couple of years ago. The neighbor offered Willie one of the puppies, and now Ahab and his son, Ishmael, live a life of luxury in Harvey's beautiful home with Willie and his family.

Several months after we got home from our trip down the river, we heard that Julian Carlton was found hiding in the basement of Taliesin after the fire had been extinguished. He had swallowed muriatic acid and died eight weeks later in the Dodgeville jail.

During the summers of our university days, Tone, Willie and I often spent weekends in the cabin on the river. Ronnie and Willie stayed there several weeks each summer, too. But last spring we had what the Old Timers called *A Hundred-Year Flood,* and the water was so high and of such power that it destroyed the cabin and washed it away. We were worried about it, but there wasn't anything we could do. After the flood was over, we drove down to the riverbank, only to find nothing left but the stove, partly buried in the sand. The tremendous current of the flood had carried away about half of the island. It will only be a matter of time until the entire island will be washed away, and the stove will sink to the bottom. No doubt, someone will find it one day in the future and wonder what a stove is doing out in the middle of the river.

The three of us stood silently, there on that riverbank, remembering one particular summer, and the great times we had on that island. We felt sadness, not only for the loss of the cabin, but because those carefree days of our boyhood were gone forever. That summer had been the most memorable summer of our lives. It was the summer when three friends retraced the journey of great explorers down the river, and when they finished the journey, they were more than friends. They were brothers.

ABOUT THE AUTHOR

Dan Bomkamp has made his home in the Wisconsin River valley all his life with the exception of his college years in La Crosse. He has been an avid hunter and fisherman his whole life. For many years he was in the sporting goods industry and began writing in the 80's for outdoor magazines. He is active in the Foreign Exchange Student program having hosted 33 boys from 13 countries over the years. Golden Retrievers have also been a big part of his life. He had at least one Golden sharing his home for 33 years. He lives in Muscoda with his cat Tigger.

His other books are: *The Adventures of Thunderfoot; More Adventures of Thunderfoot; Thanks Thunderfoot; The Gosey; Big Edna; Lost Flight; Tag; Whiteout; Spirit.*

Check out his website at www.danbomkamp.com
Or you can email him at danbomkamp@live.com